Murder at Stake
An Old School Diner Cozy Mystery

by
Constance Barker

Chapter One

"I'll need a spoon with that, sweetheart." The old farmer smiled at the tall, slender waitress as she set his bowl of split pea and ham soup on the counter.

"The name is Deloris, you old coot." She had a stern but regal look, remnants of her youthful beauty still evident in her 62-year-old face. Deloris took a step toward the silverware bin behind her as she raised an eyebrow at her daily sparring partner. "And you're starting to look more and more like that old floppy-eared hound dog of yours, Red, so I thought you might just want to lap it up with your tongue."

"Hah! She got you with a good one there, Red," chuckled Jake Carter, the burly, middle-aged owner of Carter & Son Construction Company. "Where's my Five-Alarm chili, Deloris? I ordered the same time as old Red."

No sooner had he said the words than the smoke alarm

sounded and billows of smoke started rolling out of the kitchen through the pass-through window.

"Looks like it should be just about ready, Jake," I said as I walked toward the swinging doors behind the counter. "Smoke! What's going on in there?"

My cook, Jerry Kowalski (aka "Smoke" for obvious reasons) came out of the swinging doors waving his tall chef hat to get the smoke out of his face. His young apprentice, Zack, was right behind him.

"Aw, it's nothing, Mercy. I was just teaching Zack here how to make my shepherd's pie, and I forgot all about a grilled cheese sandwich I had on the grill for his lunch."

"Ya, and it caught on fire," Zack added, to Smoke's disapproving glare.

"That's what you get for using lighter fluid instead of butter, Smoke," Red kidded, making Smoke's scowl even more intense. That comment wasn't really fair, since Smoke's cooking was always delicious.

"But it's out now, and everything is cool, ma'am," Zack added quickly. "I'll go get your chili, Mr. Carter."

The smoke dissipated, and everyone went back to their conversations. Another day in Paradise, here at the Old School Diner. I sat down in the corner booth with my inventory sheet and smiled at the minor disruption. I'm the proprietor, Mercy Howard, and this is my world. My Grandfather opened this little diner in 1964, and I just left a bad relationship and a life-consuming job as an emergency room nurse in Louisville to get back to my roots here in Paint Creek, Kentucky. Life always seemed to make sense here, so I came back last summer and bought the diner back from a city couple who decided they preferred the rat race in the big city. I guess the idyllic small town life of western Kentucky isn't for everyone.

Then suddenly the sky outside my big plate glass windows went dark, as if night had fallen in the middle of the afternoon.

"Must be one of them city-sized flying saucers hovering over Paint Creek, Jake," Red said with a grin to his conspiracy-minded friend.

"That's real funny, Red. I'm not crazy, you know. Junior's the one with all those wild ideas. Probably the government just turned on its weather-control machine. They've got satellites that can whip up hurricanes and all kinds of storms – even cause earthquakes and volcanoes, you know. Thanks, Deloris," he said as she put a large spoon down next to his bowl of chili. "I hope you didn't pull that spoon out of that beehive hairdo of yours." He smirked and kept his head down to avoid the daggers he knew would be shooting from the waitress's baby blue eyes.

"My hair is cleaner than those mitts you hold your spoon with to shovel good food into your chubby round pie hole, Jake Carter."

"I don't know," Jake dared to say. "It's been up in that

same beehive since 1956. You probably got a whole family of racoons living in there."

I had to hold back a chuckle. Deloris always kept her pen in her lofty hairdo, and was known for pulling everything from lipstick to pictures of her grandkids out of her tower of blonde hair.

Babs, the feisty round waitress who covered the booths and tables while Delores manned the counter and beverage stations, came to Jake's defense. "You leave this sweet man alone, Delores," she said with a wink to her coworker. Babs was kind of sweet on Jake, and hugged the man's neck and shoulders from behind.

Jake blushed as the somewhat stocky and slightly older spinster gave him a kiss on the cheek.

"You two should start getting along and stop teasing each other so much." She snapped her gum and brought some dirty dishes into the kitchen.

Suddenly the wind began to howl, and rain began to come down in torrents. The door opened, and Carl Jones came in, already drenched.

"Holy moly, it's gonna be a doozy of a storm out there!"

Carl, or "Jonesy" as we all called him, had a little hobby farm on the edge of town and brought me my eggs every day. He also ran the butcher shop and did some accounting during tax season. "Got nine dozen for you today, Mercy," he said, setting the box on the counter.

"That should hold me through the weekend, Jonesy. Thanks." I went behind the counter and put my glasses on to look at the invoice and initial it for him. Jonesy liked to keep perfect records for his taxes and mine.

"Here you go, Carl." Deloris handed him a mug of coffee with two spoonsful of sugar and a few drops of vanilla in it.

"Thank ya, pretty lady!" Jonesy said with his amazing and genuine smile. "Nobody makes coffee like you, Deloris."

He took a sip, and I waved for him to follow me over to my little booth.

"Hey," Jake groused, "How come Jonesy gets a free cup of coffee and Red and I have to pay. Aren't we good friends too, Deloris?"

Babs swatted him on the shoulder as she whizzed by to get the hot food in the window for another table of diners. "Delivery charge, you cheapskate. Carl made a special trip to bring those eggs here on short notice so we'd be able to make your Old School Special omelet in the morning, Jake. Coffee, Ronnie?" she asked as the owner of the hardware store walked in, wiping his feet on the mat and closing his umbrella. He nodded and sat at his usual table.

Deloris already had it on the counter, and Babs ran it out to his table and delivered a club sandwich for Missy

Daniels and pancakes for her two boys. These amazing ladies ran this place like clockwork.

Chapter Two

"So, Carl," I asked him as we looked out at the heavy rain, "I need a really big and delicious roast for Sunday dinner, and I just plain forgot to ask you about it last week. Can you help me?"

"Well, Mercy, it just so happens that I got a prime side of beef in this morning."

"Great! I'll stop by the butcher shop in the morning."

"Well, it's still in my big walk-in at the farm. I'll be cutting all day today and then grinding burger and packaging all the steaks and roasts in the morning, maybe till mid-afternoon. Why don't you just stop by after the storm dies down, and I'll carve out the tender front half of the loin for you. About 20 pounds sound about right?"

"It sure does." Carl was the sweetest man in the world, a real Paint Creek treasure, and everybody loved him. Well...almost. "How's Josie doing, Carl?"

His eyes grew concerned with a faraway look. He sighed. "Actually, that was another reason I wanted you to come out to the farm, Merse. "I was hoping you might talk to her. I don't know if she's sad or angry with me or if something happened that she won't tell me. And now this morning she said she wanted to have a talk with me tonight…I'm really afraid about what she might have to say. If I knew what was bothering her I might be able to do something to make her happy again. She's hardly ever home and stays out late doing who knows what. A couple of weeks ago she was talking about a divorce. She's been staying home the past few days now, but I'm worried." He paused to gather in his feelings and smiled at me. "She's the sunshine of my life, Mercy…"

The man looked broken, and hung his head. "My car is in the shop, Carl, but I'll get one of the girls to run me out there."

There had been rumors for a couple of months now that Josie was having an affair, but nobody seemed to know who her love interest might be. Personally, I didn't believe it. Josie Jones wasn't one of those man-crazy middle-aged cougars, and she wasn't obsessed with fashion or makeup. It's probably just some kind of mid-life crisis she's working her way through. I reached across the table and put my hand on Jonesy's just as my phone rang.

"Hello…Yup, he's right here. Do you want to talk to him? …Okay…Okay…Okay, bye."

"It was your wife, Jonesy," I told him. "She wants you to get back out to the farmhouse right away and help her close up the barn before the storm gets here."

"Roger that, Merse." He stood and gave a salute. "See you in a couple of hours." Then he turned quickly to head back out to his car, bumping straight into Pastor D'Arnaud who was also heading out the door. The two men paused briefly to exchange glares, which struck me as a little odd for such a brief and unintentional bump. Just as the door closed behind the two men the Civil Defense sirens began to wail.

"Geez, maybe Smoke started the whole town on fire this time," Red joked.

I was more alarmed, as the sound of the wind turned to a low bellow, and the heavy rain was almost horizontal. I looked at my watch to make sure it wasn't one of those "first Wednesday" one o'clock test sirens, but it was twenty minutes after 1:00, and it was Thursday. I went into my ER nurse emergency mode.

"That's a tornado warning guys. You all know Bud – he wouldn't turn that thing on unless they spotted a big twister coming our way. Everybody follow me into the cellar!" I opened the swinging doors and motioned for them to go through the kitchen to the dark narrow stairway by the back door.

Smoke and Henry, the two oldest ones there, were the hardest to convince to get downstairs. "Let's go, guys."

"A little episode of wind and rain never drove me into a cellar before, Mercy," Red said stubbornly. "I'll just ride out the storm right here on my stool."

"Me too," said Smoke. "I've been through hurricanes

at sea and tropical downpours in Nam. You get all the others downstairs, and Henry and I will man the fort here."

Red's given name was Henry, and that's how Smoke always referred to his friend. Red was about 72 and Smoke had just turned 66.

I folded my arms and stood across the counter from the two men. Zack was poking his head out of the swinging doors. "Zack, you get all the rest of these folks downstairs and comfortable, and we'll join you in a minute." He nodded, and the dozen others huddling behind him gladly followed.

"Listen, guys, I know you are both big strong brave men..." I tried not to let the sarcasm drip from my lips. "But everyone is going downstairs, or else you're going outside into that little episode of wind and rain."

They raised their eyebrows and looked at each other. "She's just joshing us, Henry. Mercy wouldn't do that."

"Wouldn't I?" I said sternly, walking to the door and grabbing the knob. "And I'm going right out there with you. There's nothing to worry about, right?"

Smoke grabbed my arm before I could pull the door open.

"You know, Henry, the last time Bud sounded the siren was when the damn broke and the whole town got flooded. Maybe Mercy's got a point."

I took the chance to build on Smoke's words.

"Besides, somebody's got to be down there to protect and comfort Delores and the others."

Slowly Red began to nod his head. I knew he had a serious crush on Delores and wouldn't mind putting his arm around her to offer a little comfort – not that she'd ever allow it, but it didn't stop me from painting the picture. As if to add an exclamation point to my demand, an awning from across the street and some large tree branches flew by the window in front of us.

"I guess we better get down there, Smoke – for the sake of the women and children."

Chapter Three

"It's about time you joined us down here, you bullheaded old fool," Delores chided Red with a look of relief in her eyes. "I thought you were going to get Mercy hurt with your stubbornness."

Zack and Jake had set out big Number 10 cans of beans and tomatoes for everyone to sit on, and I headed for a stack of rice and flour sacks, which looked a little more comfortable. Missy Daniels was down there with her two young, wide-eyed children, but most of the others were the older mid-afternoon crowd of seniors who drank coffee and tea there most days, just playing cribbage and gossiping. We sat in a circle away from the stairs as the wind continued to blow amid crashes of thunder and sounds that could have been trees snapping in two.

"I thought you made your own baked beans, Smoke, but it looks like you get them out of these big cans. I'm disappointed," Ronnie Towns said. I'm sure he was kidding, and the remark did get some smiles and helped to lower the palpable tension in the musty cellar, dimly lit with one bulb over the base of the stairs.

The light flickered as Smoke made his response. "I do make them myself. But who's got time to soak beans all night? Plus there's no room to do that in my little kitchen. I drain out all the tomato sauces and then add all the bacon and molasses and onions and secret ingredients that turn them into my own special baked beans, Ronnie. Do you make all the tools you sell at your hardware store from scratch?"

That got a laugh from the crowd just as another bolt of lightning sounded like it struck something very near.

"I hope the storm doesn't wreck up the old library," Red said. "It's a shame the way the city is wanting to tear it down and build a new brick box with no character. I studied in that old library when I was a kid, and so has everyone else who grew up here in Paint Creek. That old building is a work of art, part of the history of Paint Creek. If they want some fancy schmancy digital media center they can just run a wire to the big old basement there and put in a bunch of computers. There's lots of unused space there. Congressman Pattaway is just trying to buy our votes and get a library named after him before he bites the dust."

Babs nodded her head in agreement. "I hear you're going to go to the town council meeting next Thursday night and give them a piece of your mind, Red."

"I'm sure thinking about it, Babs. Maybe some the rest of you can come and give me a little moral support so those council members know we're serious about wanting to keep our library. Hey, Mercy, what do think about the new library idea? You're part of the younger generation. What are you, 30? 35 now?"

35! I hadn't really stopped to think much about the years passing lately, but that was a wake-up call for me. I was just 33, but 35 sounded a lot like "going on 40" to my ears, even though it wasn't that far around the corner for me.

"I love the old library, Red. We used to go and pick crab apples from the tree out back there…"

"…and I caught you kissing Billy Robinson there under that tree once too, after your Prom," Red added, much to my mortification. That got them all laughing out loud. Billy Robinson – I hadn't thought about him in years. He was a District Attorney in Knoxville now.

"All right, all right, guys. That was a long time ago."

We must have been down there for an hour, but the time passed quickly. We had forgotten all about the storm as everyone shared their memories of their time in Paint Creek.

Then the howling above us started to fade away, and it sounded like the storm was letting up. I heard footsteps upstairs, and then I could hear someone hollering.

"Mercy? Anybody here? Miss Howard? Is everybody all right?"

"Sounds like Sheriff Hayes," Zack said.

"Oh, Mercy!" Babs said excitedly. "You go up and talk to that dreamy man. He's the only man in Paint Creek under 40 who's not fat or stupid."

All heads turned, eyebrows raised, toward the chubby waitress. She just shrugged. Her remark was close to the truth. Brody Hayes was the new Sheriff, though nobody really seemed to know much about him or where he came from. He was a man of few words, and I really didn't know him – and I had no intention of getting involved with another man to mess up my new quiet life. A three-year engagement with a messy ending hadn't really given me a mindset aimed at romance. Not now. Things were just starting to get back to normal and stress-free for me.

"Anybody here?" the voice persisted.

"We're down here!" Smoke hollered back, starting up the stairs and waving for the rest of us to follow. I could hear the short "all-clear" bursts from the Civil Defense siren as we walked up the stairs to the kitchen.

Deloris whispered to me on the way up the stairs, "Be careful of that dreamy drink of water, sweetie. The tall silent type are never what they appear to be…always hiding something. I just have an uncomfortable feeling about this one, Mercy. There's gotta be a reason a man like that came to this little one-horse town. He's running away from something, mark my words." She gave me a knowing nod, and then went up ahead of me and into the dining room.

Everyone sat at the counter, and Deloris served coffee or soda to them all.

Brody put his hand on my shoulder. "Just checking out the businesses on Main Street, Miss Howard. Is everybody okay?"

"We're all fine, Sheriff, and the place seems to be in

one piece."

"Well, you're lucky. The twister touched down on the edge of town, and there's a lot of wind and lightning damage all around here too. I'm just getting ready to go out and check on the folks where the tornado was on the ground, but I thought I'd check with all the people along the avenue here first."

Babs looked at me and gave me a knowing smile, as if to say that Brody was hot for me. He was just a sheriff concerned for the townspeople.

She handed him a cup of coffee. "Sit down, Sheriff. Relax for a few minutes first."

"Well," he took a sip of the hot beverage with a lot of air to cool it off, "I really should get going…"

Then a voice came over his walkie-talkie.

"Sheriff Hayes, you better get out to the west end. There's a lot of damage here, and there's a tractor trailer on its side in the ditch. The barn at the Carl Jones farm looks like it's flattened."

Our hearts all stood still when we heard that, and we looked at each other with a sense of fear for our friend. The rain was just a drizzle now, and the sky was hazy. There were tree branches, roof shingles, and a few cautious kitties out in the street.

The sheriff fumbled for his walkie-talkie. "I'll be right there, Stan. Are you okay? Did you check on the driver of the truck? Is the road open?"

"Yes, sir, I'm fine, he's fine too. There is some standing water in that low area a quarter-mile before the bridge over Paint Creek, but nothing you can't drive through."

"I'm on my way."

Chapter Four

"My gosh." I was a little stunned by the news of the damage at Jonesy's farm. "Carl just left here right before the siren sounded. "I hope he got home in time to take cover."

"They have a storm cellar between the barn and the house, Mercy. I'm sure he and Josie are fine. I have to go."

"Sheriff..." I stopped him before he got out the door. "I told Jonesy I would go out there after the storm to pick up some meat and..."

"Talk to Josie?"

I nodded. "My car is at Arnie's waiting for a new U-joint or something like that. I was going to have Babs drive me, but, what with the storm and all we'll be busy soon, so she has a lot to do here. I was wondering..."

"Come on. You can ride with me. Grab your sweater."

The men all rushed out the door with the Sheriff and me to check on the scene. Red and Smoke jumped into Jake's big red pickup truck while Deloris and Babs started to get things in order at the diner. Everyone else went home to check on their houses and families.

The ride was quiet, except for Brody talking to his deputy from time to time.

"Just wait for me, Stan. We'll go in together to check

on Jonesy when I get there. Five minutes."

The wind damage was bad enough in town, but it was terrible once we got across Paint Creek. Some farm houses were missing parts of their roofs, cars were upended, and Charlie Dix's hay wagon was sitting on his front porch. Hazel waved cheerfully from the front yard as we drove by, and Charlie was already out with his chain saw cutting a fallen tree into firewood.

I shook my head. "A lot of damage, Brody, but at least things aren't leveled."

He just looked pensively ahead as we approached Jonesy's long driveway. Then he slowly raised his arm to point toward Jones's house below the late afternoon sun in the distance. My eye brows slowly raised and I inhaled deeply at the site. A whole section of trees in the wooded area along the farm were lying in a mangled mess on the ground, the fence was flattened, debris everywhere. The farmhouse looked in reasonably undamaged shape, but the barn…was gone.

"Oh, my God, Brody!" I instinctively put my hand on his firm shoulder and then quickly withdrew it as he turned toward me. "We have to get in there, Sheriff!"

Stan was in his car at the mouth of the driveway waiting for us and turned on his blue and red lights to lead us down the long winding path to the farmhouse. Red, Smoke, and Jake were right behind us. The minute it took for us to traverse the quarter-mile driveway seemed like an hour.

We passed a little green Rav4 about half way in or so. "It looks like Jake Junior is here. I hope he's okay." I looked back and saw Jake Sr. with his head out the window of his pick-up, staring at his son's car with a very worried look on his face.

There was red lumber from the barn strewn all over the property, ripped apart with some jagged sharp fragments sticking into the ground. The Sheriff pointed to a tree on his side of the driveway. I gasped to see a long shard of a two-by-four poking right through the trunk of a poplar tee. Large branches were blocking the way when we got close to the house. The Sheriff stopped and got out of the car. He put on his official hat and put his hands on his hips as he looked around.

"Looks like a little funnel just sat down on top of the barn and then lifted off again, or there would be even more damage around here than there is."

All that was left of the barn, which had stood a couple hundred feet in front of us, was one 8x8 corner post and a patch of concrete where Jonesy used to park his car inside the main barn doors. His car was not there. *Maybe he took shelter somewhere before he got home,* I hoped.

The big red pick-up truck pulled up next to us, and the boys all jumped out. Jake led the way, looking desperately for any sign of his son. "There!" He pointed towards a barely visible figure beginning to emerge through the haze near where the barn used to stand. He started running towards the form, which seemed to be a man with his arms raised over his head. Red and Smoke did their best to keep up with the stout construction foreman, but Jake flew like he was in an Olympic dash.

"I didn't know that man could move that fast," we heard Red say as Stan and Brody and I trotted behind them.

As we got closer I could see that it was Junior, holding his phone above his head to get some pictures of the damage. Then the three men stopped suddenly, a look of terror in their eyes. The Sheriff grabbed my arm to stop me as our eyes slowly went down to see what Junior was aiming his camera at between his feet. I let out a scream and pulled myself close to the Sheriff.

"It...it's Jonesy." Red said.

We all looked at each other with our jaws on our chest. Jonesy was lying on his back with a wooden stake sticking two feet out of his chest.

Chapter Five

Stan knelt beside him and put two fingers on Carl's carotid artery on his neck to feel for a pulse. He shook his head and then grabbed Jonesy's wrist. Then he looked up at the Sheriff and slowly shook his head.

It was clear that Jonesy was dead, but I had to see for myself. "Let me make sure," I said and took a step toward the body.

The Sheriff grabbed my arm. "Mercy, you should stand back…go wait in the car."

"Sheriff, I was an ER nurse in the city for eight years. I got this."

From his expression it was clear that he hadn't known this part of my history, and he loosened his grip on my wrist. I knelt down, but I could already tell from the dull eyes and the grey pallor of death in his flesh that it was too late for Jonesy. Our good friend had left this world. I touched his cheek and knew it must have been at least an hour ago, although the wind and rain made that hard to know for sure. I also noticed that there was no clotting around the entry point of the stake.

"He's dead as a doornail," Jake Junior said as he took my hand and pulled me to my feet with his brute strength. He continued to stand there, straddling the corpse and snapping his camera.

"What are you doing here, Junior?" Sheriff Hayes asked, quite confused. Why are you standing over Jonesy's body?"

"I'm taking pictures," Junior said, stating the obvious.

"Yes, but why? And why are you here?"

Brody looked at the ground a few feet from Junior's feet and started walking towards an object there. It was a hammer. The handle was the size of a regular carpenter's hammer, but the head on it was a sledge hammer.

Junior looked over at the object. "Looks like a six-pound sledge. Must have been in the barn before that twister blew everything all to heck. There's a hand saw over there and a pitchfork sticking out of a plank over there."

Brody took a step toward Junior and looked him straight in the eye, close up. "What are you doing here, Junior?"

Junior's head snapped up and his eyes grew wide as he began to realize that it might look a little suspicious for him to be standing over a corpse with a stake through its heart, just a few feet from a hammer.

"Now, just hold on there for a minute, Sheriff…" Junior's father stepped forward to defend his son. "Git on outa there Junior…Are you insinuating that my boy had something to do with this terrible tragedy here?" He pulled Junior away from the body.

"Not at all, Jake…"

"It's pretty obvious that the tornado ripped a board off the barn, split it down the middle longways, and sent it flying right through old Jonesy's chest."

Red stepped forward now too. "Sure looks that way to me too, Sheriff. Junior, go ahead and tell Brody what you were doing here."

Yes, please…I wanted to know that answer too.

Junior had a confused look on his face. He stepped to one side of the body and knelt by Jonesy's head. "What the heck are you guys talking about? It's obvious what happened here, but it wasn't that tornado, and it sure as heck wasn't me." He put his hands on Jonesy's mouth and started to pull back the lips.

"Whoa there, Junior!" The Sheriff grabbed the big man by the collar and pulled him to his feet.

I can't believe that, under these tragic circumstances, a small part of me swooned at the lawman's demonstration of strength.

"You can't touch the body. Even for something like this we've got to get a report from the medical examiner. What are you thinking, Junior?"

"Well, you've all got these crazy ideas about what happened. I just wanted to show you the fangs."

The men all looked at each other, and Jake slapped his forehead and shook his head. "Fangs?" Red finally said.

"Yeah. It's obvious that Jonesy here was a vampire. Why else would he have a wooden stake through his heart?"

Jake was red-faced and tried to deflect the situation as Red and Smoke giggled into their closed hands. "Junior, just tell the Sheriff why you were here."

"Well," he looked at his dad, "Pops, you know, I was bidding that job on tearing out the old loft in Earl's barn and putting in a new one. So, I was just heading back to town. I was about half a mile up the road there, and I saw that twister lift that barn clear off the ground, and then it seemed like it just blew up into a million pieces. The twister wasn't very big and started heading away from me, so I just pulled up the drive and found him lying here…just like this, with that piece of lumber sticking right out of his chest. I thought I'd take some pictures – just to help you out, Sheriff. I mean, it's not very often that we see the work of a professional vampire hunter right here in Paint Creek."

"Mmhm," Brody was sliding his thumb across his phone. "That's why you already have some shots of the scene on Facebook…to help me out, right?"

This conversation could wait. "Has anybody seen Josie? Junior, did you see her at all?"

The men all looked at each other. "I'll check the house," Smoke said, heading to the front porch.

Stan headed toward the back of the house. "I'll knock on the back door."

"Well, ya dern fools," Red said. "They got an underground a storm bunker right behind the tractor."

Sheriff Hayes was already halfway to the storm cellar, and we all followed him around the old tractor, except for Junior who stayed by the body to take more pictures. It looked like that old tractor hadn't been moved at all by the storm. It was just so odd how some things were destroyed completely and other things, including the house, were totally untouched.

There was a slanted door covered with corrugated steel sticking out of the ground, like the one on the side of my grandparent's house leading to their basement. But this door was not attached to the house. It was just in the middle of the graveled area between the house and the barn. The door started to lift open slowly as we approached, and Brody pulled it open.

"Josie!"

It was such a relief to see her, unharmed but shaken, as she emerged from the bunker with her little terrier in her arm. The dog did not yip at us, which was his usual custom, and looked a bit traumatized as he nuzzled his head in Josie's bosom.

I gave her half a hug as she looked around. She looked alarmed when she looked towards the barn, but smiled when she saw the house.

"Thank goodness the house is still standing," she said. "That old barn didn't have that many years left in it anyway." She looked around as she cuddled Skippy. "Have you seen Carl? Is he in the house? He ran out of the storm cellar to get my heart pills when there was a break in the storm. I told him not too, but I was shaking so badly he was afraid I was going to have a heart attack, Thank God the house was safe."

The woman looked at our wide eyes and long faces as we all tried to avoid her gaze. She gasped. Then Junior hollered to us.

"Hey, Sheriff! The sun is burning through pretty good

now. You better get someone to come and pick up the body, or the smell is going to have a pack of coyotes stopping by to start nibbling on old Jonesy here."

Josie dropped Skippy, who let out a little yelp and then a whimper. Brody put his arm around her waist to hold her up. Her face turned pale and she went limp.

"Stan," Brody said, "call Sylvia Chambers at the county. We need the Medical Examiner here to take care of this."

Some of the neighbor had been gathering to check on Carl and Josie when they saw the barn was missing. Florence Carwinkle from the next farmhouse saw Carl's body and was running toward her best friend, Josie, with her arms open.

"Oh, you poor dear!" The large sturdy woman hugged Josie and then led her to the house, holding the stunned widow with both arms. Skippy followed behind them as they entered the back door of the house.

"Take Miss Howard back to the diner," Brody continued, "and then come back here and help me document the scene. Guys," he said to Red, Smoke, and Jake, "see if you can find Jonesy's car."

"It's parked right behind the house, Sheriff, fine as can be."

At least Josie was in good hands, and I did have to get back. A blue-green car drove out of a wooded area way back by the driveway and headed out toward the street as we walked to Stan's patrol car. I guess neighbors were coming and going, and a crowd had gathered near the body. The Sheriff moved everyone away from the body.

Junior was just retuning from his car with a spool of yellow tape. "Here, Sheriff. It says "Caution" not "Police," but I use it around construction sites sometimes."

"Caution is all we need around this storm damage, Junior. This isn't a crime scene. Thanks."

They went about cordoning off the area while the old boys looked around and checked the house for storm damage. Stan and I drove back to Paint Creek.

Chapter Six

Word of Jonesy's death had already made its way back to the Old School diner, and just one table of regulars had trickled in for coffee and gossip so far. No doubt, more were on the way.

"How's everything going around here, Babs?" I asked as she brought a tray of freshly washed silverware out of the kitchen.

"Well, my home sweet home is fine, Mercy. No leaks or broken windows or other damage," Babs reported happily. She lived in the little apartment upstairs, above the diner. "Lollipop was hiding in the closet and might have a little PTSD. She jumped into my arms and started to purr like crazy when I went into the bedroom. Otherwise everything is fine."

It was obvious, though, that she had been shaken by the storm and by Jonesy's death, though she was doing her best to put on a brave face. Deloris gave her a hug, and a single tear started to stream down Babs's brave round face. "Jonesy was a good man, Babsy, but everything is going to be all right. I hope everything is all right at my place too."

"You two should be in good shape on the other side of town," she said to Deloris and me as she tied her apron on. "Looks like the storm just took a swoop through the west side. Just a lot of leaves and branches around here in the middle of town. The power lines are still standing."

Deloris and I both lived in the northeast corner of Paint Creek on the big hill between the town and the cemetery. "I'm worried about Wizard and Grace," I said. "Maybe I should go and check on them."

"Oh, don't be silly, Mercy," Deloris said in her brusque, confident tone. "Those darn hamsters are doing fine. They probably didn't hear a thing, and if they did they'll just cuddle up and make some babies."

"That's what I'm worried about!" I kidded. That actually brought a hint of a smile to Deloris's face as she sat down to fill salt shakers and roll silverware. "Well, I'm sure it'll be dead around here for the next hour," I continued, "but…"

"…but the whole town will be here by dinner time to exchange stories and spread gossip about poor old Jonesy," Babs added, quite correctly.

"I'd better get the roast in the oven for Smoke," Deloris said, as she got up from the big corner booth and headed for the kitchen. "He won't be back until the CSI team is done and gone."

"CSI? Babs asked, a little befuddled. "Why would a crime unit be out there for a storm, Deloris?"

She shook her head and turned back to the dining room from the swinging doors. "The man's got a stake through his heart, woman. Doesn't that sound a little odd to you?" Then she disappeared to deal with the roast.

Her remark rattled me a little bit. It might be worth investigating, I thought…but of course it was a freak accident caused by the tornado. Right? Babs and I stared at each other as a chill froze us in place at the thought, for a moment.

"It looked like the storm blew that wooden stake to me, Babs."

"I swear," Babs said, pouring salt through the funnel into the shakers, "that woman's brain is going to turn to mush from listening to Jake's wild stories."

That made me feel better, and we got the diner ready for the dinner rush. I went outside with the big push-broom to sweep away the leaves and debris from the sidewalk out front. There was an eerie stillness, and the sky shone a hazy yellow as the mid-afternoon sun tried to burn off the mist left by the storm. I looked across the wide main street at Brandi's Donut House and was glad I hadn't yet installed the new awning I had been planning for my outdoor tables this summer. *Poor Brandi,* I thought.

Just then she came out of her shop with a big smile and wave. She cupped one hand by her mouth. "Quite the storm, huh, Mercy?"

I nodded. It was uplifting to see her happy mood despite the loss of her beautiful awning. It seemed that she hadn't heard about Jonesy yet.

"Here comes the Ladies' Aid Society." An hour had passed, and Bab's was looking out of the big front window as Hattie Harper and Sandy Skitter rode up on their bicycles. The two old spinsters were rarely seen apart.

Deloris looked up. "Yep, looks like Elvira Gulch and Tinker Bell are coming to bless us with their presence. Audrey and Eva should be along shortly."

Elvira Gulch was the old woman on the bike in Kansas who became the Wicked Witch in the Wizard of Oz, and Hattie did resemble her when she rode up on her bicycle in her black pillbox hat with a drooping black flower on it. She was the undisputed leader of the ladies' group that came in at least one afternoon a week and every Saturday. Sandy was her big-eyed yes-woman, sweet as honey but not very bright. Audrey was married to Hank Albright, president of the bank, and Eva Parsons was a lonely widow, getting heavier and more bitter every day, it seemed. They called themselves the Paint Creek Sewing Circle and Book Review Charity Club, but mostly they were referred to by the locals as the Ladies' Aid Society. Smoke called them the Soap Opera and Gossip Club, but they did take on a lot of charitable and civic endeavors for the community.

Babs knew they would want the big booth in the corner, and she quickly snatched up the last tray of salt shakers and silverware from her corner "office" as the ladies walked in. Predictably, Audrey and Eva followed a couple of minutes later.

"Bring some ice water for the ladies and iced tea with

lemon for me," Hattie ordered Babs. "Put it all on my check. And bring two more glasses – Vonnie and Emma should be joining us."

"Yes, ma'am!"

"Oh – and bring me three cubes of sugar. Your teaspoons don't measure properly."

"Right away, Hattie."

"And I'd like a piece of that cherry cobbler in the pie case, Babs," Sandy requested. "It looks delicious!"

"No food, Sandy. You're getting a little porky around the middle again." Hattie gave her a stern look. "It took me three months of having you run behind my bicycle last summer to get rid of your extra flab. I don't have that kind of time to waste. Unless you don't want to be my personal secretary any more… Besides, this is a business meeting. We don't need your fork clinking and you chomping away and scarfing down pie while we're trying to conduct a meeting."

Sandy looked alarmed and turned a ghostly pale and then bright red. "Just the water, please, Babs."

More diners began to file in, and the counter was filling up as the men returned from Jonesy's farm.

Chapter Seven

"I got your table all set, fellas," I told the group holding out my right arm toward the long table on the opposite end of the dining room. The retired guys would sit at the big table on the end and comment on the passersby and other customers – particularly the young women walking by and the old birds in the corner booth. Smoke had a hurried look on his face as he followed Jake through the front door.

"Don't worry, old man," Deloris told him as she poured water into the coffee maker behind the counter. "Your beef has been roasting nicely at 350 for an hour, and it will be a tender medium rare or so by 5 o'clock."

Zack had returned a while ago through the back door and poked his head into the pass-through window. "And the gravy and chili and soup are all warmed up in the steam table, and all the greens and vegetables are cut and prepped, Smoke. Just sit down with the guys and let me handle it for a while."

Smoke looked at me, a bit of skepticism in his eyes, but I gave him the go-ahead nod and he sat at the end of the table, closest to the kitchen. "Don't mind if I do!"

Red followed a moment later, moving slowly and pulling his little red hand cart behind him. It held his oxygen tank, and he had the tubes leading to his nostrils. I guess the shock of Jonesy's death had really gotten to him. He didn't use the tank very often.

"Red!" I went to help him through the threshold, but he would have no part of it.

"I don't need any help, Mercy. This thick air after the storm is just so muggy, it's hard for these old lungs to get any oxygen out of it. I'll be just fine in a minute, now that I'm inside." He sat at the big end table with the other men.

The men all sat on the far side of the table along the wall so they could see the action in the diner, and Delores set down a pot of hot coffee and a pitcher of iced tea with slices of lemon peeking through the sides and floating on top. Babs was right behind her with a tray of cups and glasses.

"Here you go, boys," she said with her bright smile. "We'll bring out some appetizers in a while."

Smoke was on the end of the table closest to the kitchen, then Jake and Red. Jake Junior, his dad's 25-year old son and partner in the family construction company, had returned with the guys too. Pete Jenkins, who had a farm not far from Jonesy's, was with them now too. He was a quiet, single man, about 40, and always stayed pretty much to himself. But this horrific event was enough to bring him out. Stan Doggerty, Brody's 28-year-old deputy, walked in the door and joined the table.

"Deputy Dawg!" Jake Junior greeted him. "Where's your boss? I thought he left when the rest of us did."

"He's not far behind, Junior. He said he just wanted to

cruise the streets of town a little bit to make sure things were okay first. He'll be by shortly."

"Poor old Jonesy," Junior said as Stan took a chair near the end of the table, saving the head of the table for the Sheriff. "I always suspected he was a vampire, but I didn't know we had a Van Helsing here in town to do him in!"

And so it began…

The others turned toward the stout spitting image of his father.

"What are you talking about, Jughead?" Red inquired. "Who said anything about Jonesy being a vampire?"

"Hey! Don't call my boy Jughead," Jake protested.

"Why not, Jake? You do. Heck, I thought that was his name until I got his graduation announcement when he was 19."

"That's different. He's my boy, I can call him what I want, Red. Besides, everybody calls him Junior, which means his name is the same as mine, you old goat."

Red just shrugged. "I don't know. I figured Jake might be your middle name. He could be Jughead Junior…"

Jake started to get up from his chair, but Smoke pulled him back down with a hand on his shoulder. Jake settled down.

Smoke liked to encourage Junior with his entertaining

ideas. "So tell us about your vampire theory, Junior."

Junior looked surprised. "Well, what the heck else could it be? Somebody put a wooden stake through his heart. Obviously, that has to be because he's a vampire. Duh!"

His father shook his head, a little embarrassed at his son's silly theory. "He was no vampire, Junior…"

"Of course, he wasn't," Smoke added. "The tornado put the stake though his chest, not a vampire hunter." Smoke shook his head, and most of the other men let out a quiet round of laughter.

Jake waved the laughter down. "Whoa, whoa there, guys. It may not have been a vampire hunter who done him in, but it wasn't that twister either."

The men looked at each other, waiting for Jake Sr.'s theory. "It's all part of that government conspiracy I've been telling you about…"

"I think I'm going to need a beer, Smoke," Red whispered to his friend. "You still got some in your tapper back there?"

Smoke always made room for a small keg in the back refrigerator, and liked to sip on the suds throughout the day in the hot kitchen. Just enough to keep cool and refreshed.

Jake continued. "…You know they've been putting mind control drugs in the meat at his butcher shop for months now. Maybe Jonesy told them he wanted them to cut it out, and they did this as a warning to anyone else who tried to stop them."

The front door opened again, and Sheriff Hayes stepped in. Maybe now we could get some of the real story, now that they've had time to examine the scene.

Chapter Eight

Rumors and oddball theories were flying through the diner as the Sheriff took his seat at the head of the long table.

Babs set down a steaming bowl of chili & cheese dip surrounded by chips and crackers and a platter of fresh cut veggies. "This should keep you guys satisfied long enough for Zack to fill the orders for the other diners. Then you can order something more substantial after that, guys"

"You can put that rabbit food on the other end of the table, Babsy, and slide that chili dip down this way," Red told her with a bit of the old drill sergeant that he used to be in his attitude. "Mercy, you can take those carrots and celery stalks home for those guinea pigs of yours. We don't need them 'round here."

"Slide them my way, Babs," Brody said with a gentlemanly smile. "That's just the snack I need right now."

"This special meeting of the Paint Creek Sewing Circle and Book Review Charity Club will come to order," Hattie said from her booth. "Slide over ladies; make room for the rest of our members."

Emma Vanderjack and Vonnie D'Arnaud, the preacher's wife, just walked by the window and were coming in the front door. Emma didn't look like her usual talkative self, and Vonnie seemed even quieter and more withdrawn than usual. I swear I've scarcely heard that woman ever say a word. They headed for the corner booth, which held the six ladies perfectly.

"I hope those old hens don't yack too loud," Red said as he took the oxygen tubes off and rubbed the whickers on his chin.

"Well, they've got important things to discuss," Smoke said with fake indignation. "After all, there's been a lot of calamity in that Kardashian household this week, I'm sure, and they'll have to stick their noses into everyone's business here in Paint Creek too."

"Well, I hadn't thought about that," Red chuckled. "I suppose you're right. Babs, bring us out a pitcher of beer from Smoke's keg back there. I really need a cool one right now."

"Why, I don't know what you're talking about, Red Barber," Babs said, trying to see Sheriff Hayes out of the corner of her eye. "This is a respectable diner, not a saloon, ya know."

Brody just rolled his eyes. "It's okay, Babs. Just put it in a china pitcher instead of a glass one so that people can't see it, and give us some coffee mugs to pour it in. Honestly, I could use a little relaxer right now too. It's been a stressful day."

Smoke and Red raised their eyebrows at each other and did a fist bump.

I was curious about the scene at the farm and walked

up to Brody. "So what was it Sheriff? Vampire slayers, or NSA goons trying to protect the government's mind control program?"

"Huh? Uh…what?" He looked at me like I'd lost my mind and nearly fell off his chair.

I smiled, and subtly nodded my head toward the gang. He began to get the idea.

"Oh, yeah…heh heh. Well, it was quite the scene, a lot of damage and a pretty macabre sight, what with the body and all. You know that – you were there, Mercy. Josie seemed to be taking it pretty hard, though. I looked in on her and Florence before I left." Brody pulled a chair over from the next table, and I sat across from the men.

There had been a lot of gossip and speculation about Josie and Carl's marriage falling apart, and the ladies in the corner seemed to think she was having an affair, from the talk I'd overheard the past few weeks. But I don't know…she didn't really seem the type, and Carl was such a kind man and devoted husband.

"Is she doing all right? Is Florence still there with her?"

Pete Jenkins piped up. "Oh, yeah…Florence Carwinkle is still there, and Josie's sister is coming in from Pigeon's Roost later tonight."

I nodded.

"Holy macaroons, look at that!" Jake was looking at a

picture on Junior's phone, and the other men were all leaning into see it. "I saw that thing when it was sticking out of old Jonesy's chest, but it sure looks mighty sharp and wicked after they pulled it out."

"Pass that over this way, Junior," I said with my hand extended across the table. "Let me take a look."

Brody swung his head toward me quickly. "Oh, Miss Howard, I don't know. I know you're a nurse, but this was a pretty gruesome scene, especially after the ME pulled the stake out. Lots of blood and…"

I gave him a scoffing glance. "Don't worry about it, Sheriff. I know I'm just a weak-hearted little female, but I think I can handle it. I've seen plenty of gunshot wounds and stabbing victims. I'm, well, a scientist."

He folded like a pair of duces in the World Series of Poker. "Oh! Well, of course you are, Mercy…uh, Miss Howard. I wonder what else I don't know about you."

"Probably quite a lot, since we've only met a handful of times, Brody…uh, Sheriff."

I took the phone from Junior's hand and held it so Brody and I could both see it. The bloody stake was lying on the ground next to a yellow evidence marker with the number "1" and a yardstick that showed it to be 27 inches long.

"From the blood on it, it looks like about 10 inches of it penetrated and 17 inches were left sticking out of his chest," I said. "The sharp end is curled up like it hit something hard." I gave the Sheriff a curious look.

"Yeah, we figure it was sticking out of his back when he fell backwards onto the ground, The point got smashed some."

For some reason I was fascinated by that bloody stake. It was about two inches by two inches on the wide end – like a two-by-four split lengthwise – and then it tapered to a jagged, splintered point. "Why the evidence marker, Brody? Is this a crime scene?"

"Oh, no, Miss…"

"Just call me Mercy, please."

"Sure, Mercy. Nah, we didn't bring in a team. I just had Stan throw one down along with a yardstick for the official record. The medical examiner is pretty professional and picky too. You know Sylvia. We like to document accidents too. Just standard procedure."

I thumbed through Junior's other photos of the scene and stopped on one of Jonesy on his back with the stake sticking straight up towards the camera. "You must have been straddling the body when you took this one, Junior."

"Sure was, Mercy. I took it right before you and the Sheriff got there. And Sheriff, this was no accident. Jonesy was murdered plain and simple."

"That's right," his dad agreed. "Government thugs."

"Nope, vampire hunters."

"Guys," Brody said, "This was just a tragic accident caused by a big tornado."

I wasn't so sure of that anymore. "Brody, how fast would that stake have to be flying to go all the way through a man's chest?"

"At least a hundred, I'd guess. Why?"

"Well, at a hundred miles an hour, it would either break his ribs, front and back, or if it went between his ribs it would keep going a lot deeper than 10 inches."

"I don't know…"

"And look at this picture here." I showed him one from a few feet away from the body with the stake sticking out. "Do you see that? The part of the stake sticking out of his body isn't bloody at all above the entry point."

"So…what does that mean?"

"Well, if he fell on his back after the stake went in, the ground would have pushed it up at least a little. There should be some blood on the stake above the wound here…but there isn't."

"Well, the ground was probably soft from all the rain, Mercy."

"No, it's baked hard around the barn, real hard…and the tip isn't muddy, it's bent. And look here…" I flipped to the picture taken directly above the stake. "There's an impression on the top end of the stake, like it was hit with a sledge hammer."

"Bam!" Junior raised his fist into the air in triumph. "A vampire hunter pounded a wooden stake through his heart with that little sledge hammer by Jonesy's dead body! Pour me another beer, Pops."

Chapter Nine

"Gracie! You leave him alone. It's Wizard's turn in the wheel! You just sleep in it anyway."

I was trying to get an earring in while walking in one high heel as I went over to scold my alpha-female hamster. "Now you behave there, young lady!"

That wasn't likely. Grace was always ruling the roost over my sweet Wizard. He has a little dark line of fur on his forehead, and although it doesn't really look like a lightning bolt to anyone else, he became my little "Wizard" the moment I saw him at the pet store.

I needed a little life around the house when I moved back to Paint Creek last year, and the green thumb skipped a generation. Hopefully these little critters will fare better than my houseplants have in the past. The best part about hamsters is that I don't feel totally insane when I talk in the house…I can just talk to them instead of myself. They've helped me work through a lot of issues.

"Okay, guys…sorry, Gracie, but 'guys' is a perfectly fine non-gender-specific term in the plural form, so don't look so offended. Anyway, I have to get ready to go to Jonesy's memorial service at the church, so just be good. I'll chop up an apple slice and a floret of broccoli for you two, so share nice. Your water looks good."

I wobbled back to my other shoe and looked at myself in the hall mirror on the way to the kitchen. "Why, thank you, Wizard! I do look quite lovely today, don't I?" It was just a blue knee-length dress, but my hair was actually hanging with a little bounce in my usually tangled natural waves. "Okay, okay…I'll get your food! Just be patient. Babs will be here to pick me up in a few minutes! Ouch!" The darn latch on the cage bit me when I opened it to get the tiny bowl for their food. Okay…it was a pickle jar cover. *I'd better stop at the hardware store and get a new latch one of these day.*

No sooner had I set the chopped meal in the hamster cage than the doorbell rang. I let out a little sigh of exasperation and looked toward the refrigerator in the kitchen. I was hoping to have a nibble or two of the Deloris's carrot cake that I brought home from the diner last night. I muttered to myself. "No rest for the weary. I didn't need that snack anyway." Then I headed for the door. "Be right there, Babs!"

I pulled open the front door, still looking down at my dress while tugging it down and brushing out the folds of fabric on my not-so-flat tummy. "I'm almost ready, Babs, but do you think the way the skirt hangs makes it look like I have a big butt? Maybe I should change…" I looked up and immediately turned to stone. My jaw dropped, and a cold chill ran through my body. I wasn't looking at Babs…it was the face of Brody Hayes. I tried to speak, but only guttural utterances came out. I wanted to shrink into a little hamster and run away.

"I think you look perfectly lovely from head to toe, Mercy. Babs said she was having car trouble and asked me to pick you up. I thought she would have told you, but…"

"But she didn't…no. Come in, Sheriff. I am so…I just…I didn't…"

Brody smiled, but not with a cocky "gotcha" smile. "No worries, Mercy. I'm just glad that guys don't have to go through all the preparation and anxiety that women have to deal with every time they leave the house."

I was transfixed by his blue eyes and couldn't look away, even though I was sure that I was allowing him to totally read my mind and tap into all my insecurities and improper stirrings. "So, you think this is suitable for a memorial service, Brody?"

I guess that gave him permission to slide his eyeballs all up and down my body. It made me a little self-conscious of my imperfections, and I swear I could feel the caress of his gaze rubbing against my skin. He looked a little longer than necessary for a quick inspection. Then he smiled again, but this time we both looked away from each other's eyes and snapped back to reality.

"It's very appropriate, Mercy." He looked around my living room. "Nice place! Are you ready to go?"

"Yes…yes, I am. Do I need a wrap?"

"Nope. It's a beautiful Spring day. But churches can be kind of dank, so maybe bring something light."

Chapter Ten

The brand-new Incarnation Church was built on a beautiful lot with rolling hills just two or three miles outside of town. The parking lot was nearly full, as much of the town had turned out to remember Jonesy. The first car I saw as Brody drove toward an open parking spot was Babs's little Chevy Cruz. The words in my mind worked their way to the back of my tongue, and I muttered through my teeth. "Why, that devious little matchmaker…"

"Hm? What's that?" Brody asked.

"Oh…nothing, Brody. I was just noticing that it looks like Babs made it after all. I saw her car back there. I wonder if she picked up Deloris…" I put my Egyptian print silk scarf over my shoulders. It was wide enough to double as a shawl and accented my plain blue dress nicely. I opened my door before Brody could have a chance to walk around and open it for me. There was something about being a little dressed up and walking next to a handsome man that did make this feel like a date. But it was also uncomfortable, as I knew tongues would soon be wagging once we walked into the service together.

"Hidee ho there, neighbors!"

It was Junior with his dad, Jake, driving past us a little too fast and zooming his dad's pickup truck into a stall in front of us. Normally I would have waved and kept on walking, but not this time. "Let's wait for them,

Brody. We can all go in together." Some tongues would still wag, but at least I would have some plausible deniability.

Babs was sitting next to Deloris in the third row, and she turned around and waved for us to join her. *Great.* Then she whispered loudly.

"Come on! Come on!"

By now she had brought everyone's attention to us, and all heads turned including the Ladies' Aid group in the front row on the other side of the aisle. Hattie immediately turned to Sandy and started whispering.

"You two go on ahead," Junior said. "Me and Pops will sit in the back here so we can be the first ones out and get a good place at the diner as soon as you open it up afterwards."

Swell. That's where I had intended to sit too, but we made our way past the entire congregation and joined Babs and Deloris. Smoke and Red were right in front of them. Smoke raised his eyebrows at us twice and Red snickered. *Real mature, guys.* I couldn't wait for this to be over.

Pastor D'Arnaud walked out to the pulpit in ceremonial garb, and the congregation grew quiet. His wife Vonnie was seated at the edge of the sanctuary with her head down and hands in white gloves folded in her lap. I looked around for Josie Jones, but couldn't find her.

As the Pastor began his eulogy I whispered to Babs, "Where's Josie?"

She shook her head and shrugged. "Not here!"

That seemed very odd to me. Either she was an emotional wreck, or she didn't care at all. Either way, it was still unusual for the widow not to show up for her husband's memorial service, even if they were having problems. She probably wanted to avoid this big crowd, and I was sure she'd show up for the burial tomorrow.

Pastor D'Arnaud seemed a little off too. He did a lot of scripture reading and prayers, but had almost nothing to say about Carl Jones, the man – our friend and neighbor. Surely, there were many good things he could say about the man.

The pastor and his wife were at the door to greet everyone as we filed out of the church.

"Nice sermon, Pastor," I lied. "Why don't you and Vonnie stop at the diner and let us provide your dinner today? I'm sure the people would all be happy you see you there."

"That's kind of you, Mercy, but Vonnie and I have to get to the butcher shop."

He was quite terse and then moved on to shake hands with Brody and Red and the others behind me. *Butcher shop?* Jonesy ran the butcher shop, so it's probably not even open. Vonnie didn't even make eye contact and just swayed like a little girl with her hands behind her back. Her totally inward behavior made me wonder if she was battered…I had seen a lot of Battered Wife Syndrome in the hospital. But of course, that was impossible…the Pastor was a wonderful man.

Brody was quiet, reading the messages on his phone, until we got to the car. It seemed that he had something on his mind. He stood by my locked door and looked at the sky, using one hand as a visor to block the sun. Then he looked at me.

"The Medical Examiner agrees with you, Mercy." He pushed the button on his key fob to unlock my door and opened it. "It looks like we've got a murder to solve."

Chapter Eleven

Tongues had been wagging with all kinds of crazy theories about Jonesy's unusual death, especially once the town became overrun with investigators and crime scene teams from three counties…and this morning's Calhoun Bi-Weekly Tribune confirmed that it was a murder.

"It's been pretty obvious from the first day that they're looking at this as a murder," Red told Jake, folding the newspaper and sliding it down the counter for other guests. "All these high-falutin medical teams in white lab coats swarming over Jonesy's farm, and these guys in suits instead of Smokey uniforms aren't just here for the freak show of a guy with a stake through his heart."

"That's what I've been telling you all along," Jake agreed, looking around at the suits and lab coats in three of the tables by the windows. He lowered his voice. "It's a government conspiracy, all because of those mind control drugs they were injecting into the meat at Jonesy's butcher shop." Then, with his eyes conspicuously on the investigation team, he cupped his hand between his mouth and Red's ear and whispered, "And these are all government agents, here to cover up their little science experiment. They're looking for ways to pin the murder on some poor soul from Paint Creek so we never find out that they were the ones who done him in when he threatened to blow the whistle."

"Well, that might make a good movie, Jake, and I

wouldn't be surprised to find out that they planted some kind of worm in your brain to control *your* mind. But Junior's story about vampires is more likely than your idea. It's pretty simple, really – Josie didn't show up for his memorial service or his funeral, and nobody knows where she is. Everybody knows they weren't getting along, and Florence said that some nights she could hear them arguing clear over at her place across a couple of acres. The wife knocked him out and pounded that stake through his heart to make it look like the tornado did it…or else she had her secret lover do it. That's what happened. Mystery solved."

Deloris topped off Red's coffee and set down another frosty coffee cup of ice cold beer for Jake. "At least someone around here still has a lick of sense. No offense, Jake, but your wild stories are just too far-fetched for people with a normal brain."

Jake snapped his head toward the tall waitress. "Are you saying that my brain…"

Babs put her hand on his shoulder and rubbed his strong upper arm. "She's saying that your brain is way above normal, Jake. Most average people just can't latch onto your big ideas." She winked at Deloris and brought a tray of dirty dishes to the kitchen.

Deloris shook her head a little but went along with her friend. "That's right, Jake. Your big brain is just too far ahead of the rest of us, so we have to try to come up with everyday explanations we can comprehend with our tiny little pea brains."

The front door opened to a petite woman in a blue dress walking backwards with a cameraman focused on her. It was Talia Jones, the news lady from TV.

"We're here at the Old School Diner in Paint Creek, where friends of the murder victim, Carl Jones, are going about their lives in the wake of this horrific crime. Let's see what the locals can tell us about this crime and the neighbor they lost so tragically."

She was heading towards Jake at the counter, who had turned his stool around to see what was going on. Afraid that the town's sanity would be judged by Jake's story of government intrigue, Deloris pointed toward me. "That's the owner, Mercy Howard," she said. "She's good friends with Sheriff Hayes, so she probably knows more than anybody else."

I gave Deloris a look of consternation from where I stood at the end of the counter, but quickly plastered on a smile as the camera turned towards me. *Did I comb my hair? I should have worn lipstick. Well frick...*

"Miss Howard, how has this murder affected your small community in Paint Creek?"

What did she say? In a nervous self-conscious moment I forgot to listen and was caught totally off guard. I felt like I had slipped into a dream world, but did my best to appear like a normal human being. I put on one of those concerned furrowed-brow smiles like people give you at funerals.

"I...uh...Carl was a wonderful man and a good friend.

He was my butcher and my accountant, and he was always kind as well as very good at everything he did. He was a big part of our lives, and we can't believe he's gone."

"Is it true that he was planning to run for Mayor in the fall election? Would the town have elected him?"

What? That was something I had never heard before. Was Bud retiring? I'm sure I had a confused look on my face, but fortunately Sheriff Hayes just walked through the door, and the crew from Channel 4 Live Action News quickly pounced on the uniformed man in the tall hat.

Brody stopped in his tracks, knowing he was trapped. I mouthed "Thank you!" to him as Talia attacked.

"Sheriff, what's the latest on the unusual murder? Do you have anyone in custody? A principal suspect? Or at least a person of interest in the case?"

Brody did his best to make his non-answers sound like they were substantial until Talia and her crew followed the investigative team of detectives and crime scene inspectors out the door. I had moved to the small window booth, and Brody joined me there, hailing Babs for a cup of coffee on the way. It seemed like every head in the diner turned to look at us. Some smiled slyly while others began to whisper to their neighbor without taking their eyes off us.

Babs wasn't so shy. "Here's your black coffee, Sheriff. Would your lady friend like anything?" She smiled smugly at me.

I gave her the evil eye, and she bounced away proudly.

"Maybe I should sit somewhere else, Mercy…"

"Just pay no attention to these gossip hounds, Brody. We both know there's nothing going on between us."

He put his head down and drummed the table with his fingers. Then he looked at me.

"What is it, Brody?'

"Well…it's just…maybe they're not altogether wrong. Maybe there's a part of me that would like to get closer to you…"

Deloris sneaked up from behind Brody and set a raspberry tea on the table for me. "And we all know what part that is, don't we, Sheriff?"

"Deloris!" I said, quite aghast as she made her getaway.

Brody's face turned beet red, and he started to rise to his feet.

I reached across the table and grabbed his wrist. "Sit."

He slowly obeyed and started to apologize.

"Just never mind Deloris and the others," I reassured him. "It's none of their business what either of us think or feel. I mean, after all, there aren't too many people around this town in their 30s with a college education and who've seen a little bit of the world outside of these city limits. It's only natural that we would be comfortable talking to each other."

I hoped I hadn't said too much. I didn't want to lead him on…or myself, either…but it did seem to settle him down. I had a lot of great friends in Paint Creek, but none I could discuss Shakespeare or macro-economics with. It was nice to have a broad, rational mind I could connect with at times.

We talked for a couple of hours, wrapped in our own little bubble, almost unaware of the diners around us. Eventually, as dinner time came and went, all of the guests had trickled out. Even Deloris and Smoke were gone now, and Babs said her goodbye as she went out the back door to the stairway to her apartment.

Brody looked at his watch, grinning broadly. "Wow…time flies when you're…"

"…having a great time," I finished, a warm smile on my face. "Stay a while. I want to pick your brain about Jonesy. I know you can't tell me much, but…"

"I'll tell you anything, Mercy. Your insights have already helped to move the investigation ahead. I could use your help. But, you have to be sworn to secrecy on everything I tell you."

"Scout's honor," I said, crossing my heart.

"I think scouts do something like this," he said,

holding up his right hand like he was taking an oath, with his thumb holding down his pinky nail and three fingers rising straight up.

"So…tell me. Where has your investigation led you?"

"Well, we've pretty much ruled out vampires," he began with a smile.

"Junior will be disappointed!"

Then he got a more serious look. "Yeah, he might be. It seems that his dad's theory about mind control drugs in the meat actually began with Junior. A lot of people saw Carl and him arguing about it at the butcher shop three or four times in the past few weeks."

I was confused. "Why on earth would he come up with an idea like that? I assumed that Jake had just been watching too much cable television lately."

"Well, Mr. Jenkins said that some federal USDA inspectors had been by the butcher shop, following up on some mad cow threat in southern Indiana. They were taking some needle biopsy kind of samples from the cuts of beef, and Junior figured they were injecting something. When he asked them what they were doing, they just told him something like, 'You didn't see anything. We were never here.' Jake figured they were seeing if they could control his mind with their Jedi mind trick, and then Jake…"

"Jake put his theory together from there. Interesting."

"So, we're going to bring Junior in tomorrow and

interrogate him."

"What!" I gasped. "Brody, Junior is a little eccentric, but he's not a killer! There's no need to bring him in."

"Maybe so, maybe no. But somebody killed Carl Jones. So just tell me who the killer in town is, and I'll go and arrest him."

He had a point. "Well, I know somebody killed Jonesy, Brody. But I really don't think it was Junior. Any other suspects?"

"Everybody in town. If you're asking who else had the motive and opportunity, right now that would be Josie."

Oh, crud.

Chapter Twelve

Jake was inconsolable at the diner the next morning.

"Why are they bringing my boy in for questioning? We were all there – there's no way he had anything to do with polishing off old Jonesy. They were always real good friends. They even went bowling together in Calhoun every month or so."

Red patted his buddy on the shoulder. "It's just routine, Jake. You know how it is…the lawmen have to make it look like they're doing something, so they make a show out of making the rest of us look like criminals. Then they pick the one the newspapers hate the most, arrest 'em, give 'em a phony trial, and hang 'em."

Babs punched Red in the shoulder hard enough to make him holler.

"Don't pay any attention to that old gas bag, Jake. He's right that it's just routine, though. Junior was the first one on the scene after it happened. He's the one who found Jonesy's body lying there, so they want to get all the details they can from him, that's all. Now don't you worry." She kissed Jake on the cheek and then grabbed a piece of Red's shoulder with her thumb and forefinger, giving it a good twist.

"Yeowtch!" Red gave Babs a look, but he didn't say a word, knowing he'd get something worse if he did.

It was hard to watch Jake, on the verge of tears and not

touching his donut or his coffee. I walked to the counter and grabbed his keys.

"Come on, Jake. We're going to the courthouse."

"But, Sheriff said I couldn't go with Junior. I don't know…"

"I'll take care of the Sheriff, Jake. Deloris, put his coffee in a go-cup with a lid, and give me a cup too."

Jake stood up eagerly and sniffled back a tear. "Give me the keys, Mercy. I'll drive; it's a long ways to Calhoun, and my truck's a stick."

I had to smile. Calhoun is the county seat of McLean County, a whole seven miles from Paint Creek. "Not a problem, Jake. I won the Powder Puff Derby with a stick at the County Fair six years ago…drove a four-on-the-floor all through nursing school too. I think I can survive the ten-minute drive.

I left my purse in the truck and told Jake to empty his pockets. "We can't take pocket knives or any other metal through the entrance, Jake…they'll just confiscate it…um, they'll take it away and keep it. Leave everything here."

"What about my Budweiser belt buckle, Mercy?"

"They'll wand us at the door, so you don't have to take it off."

"That's good, 'cuz without my belt my pants would end up around my ankles."

Thanks for the image, Jake.

I walked up to the desk and asked for the Sheriff.

"Sheriff Hayes is busy, ma'am. You can make an appointment across the lobby. Justine at the Register of Deeds office will be happy to help you."

The uniformed officer didn't seem to understand. "Just tell him Mercy Howard and Jake Carter are here to see him."

"But…"

I hollered toward the double doors at the end of the hall. "Bro-DEEEE!"

That seemed to get everybody's attention, including the Sheriff's. He opened the door enough to stick his head through and waved for us to come.

"What are you doing here, Mercy? We're just about to start the interrogation."

"I know. That's why we're here. Jake and I are going to observe through the one-way glass."

"But…"

"Come on, Jake." I had been through the courthouse

many times with my uncle, who had been an attorney when I was growing up. I knew the interrogation room was right around the corner. We went through the door to the small hallway gallery adjacent to the interrogation room. There was a row of eight or ten wooden chairs with a raised row of chairs behind it, but we opted to stand by the window, where we could see Jake Junior and a few others inside the room. We got inquisitive looks from the two men and one woman who were already at the window.

Brody introduced us. "This is Mercy Howard, a medical trauma expert who was at the scene. She's, uhhh, been deputized for this case. And this is Jake's dad, Jake Senior. Umm…Junior's family doctor recommended that he be here. These are detectives Ransford, Demetrius, and Hennessey."

Nice job, Brody! You're a natural-born liar. Maybe too natural…

"Tell my boy I'm here, Sheriff, will ya?"

Brody nodded and joined several others in the interrogation room across the table from Junior, who was looking very pale and nervous. After the Sheriff whispered to him he smiled and waved at us through the mirror.

"Hi, Pops!"

We could hear him just fine through the little speaker above the glass.

Jake looked a lot better now, and let out a relaxing exhale. "So, why didn't you tell me that Doc Jessup wanted me to be here, Mercy? Here, I thought we were just kind of barging in like a couple of unwelcomed guests."

I blushed a little and just shrugged, not wanting to blow Brody's fairly convincing cover story.

A very tall, statuesque, and well-coifed woman in a fashionable tan business suit walked into the interrogation room, her Prada heels clicking on the marble floor as she walked to the chair directly across from Junior. Her shoulder-length blonde hair bounced like a model's hair in a shampoo commercial as she floated through the room. This was a sophisticated big-city woman, maybe from the state Attorney General's office in Frankfort. Junior looked like he had never seen a woman like her before, and he probably hadn't. Her male secretary followed her, got her seated, and then sat in a chair in the corner of the room and opened his laptop. She nodded at the court reporter and cameraman to indicate that the interrogation was beginning.

She put on her reading glasses and opened a folder in front of her. "Mr. Carter? I'm Alexandra Witherspoon, an attorney for the State of Kentucky. Do you know why you're here today?"

Junior was wide-eyed. His face reddened and his hand started to shake as he tried to answer. "Um, yes sir…ma'am…sir. I think so. Sheriff said he wanted to talk to me about old Jonesy getting killed out at his farm the other day. That's right, ain't it?"

She licked her fingertip and turned to the next page of her notes. "Do you know what a deposition is, Mr. Carter?"

"Uh…some kind of yoga position? Or…or, maybe some kind of drug from the drugstore? No! Jonesy's death position was on his back. Is that what you meant?"

"Mr. Carter…"

Junior was desperate to look smart in front of these people and was thrown off by the pop quiz. "Or did you say depth perception? 'Cuz I learned about that when I learned how to drive the big semi-trucks. That means, like, if you can tell if things are close or far away."

He seemed proud as he looked around at the stunned faces of the others around the table.

"Yes…that's right, Mr. Carter."

It was nice of Ms. Witherspoon not to embarrass Junior.

"Today we're going to ask you about things you saw, um, close up or at a distance, and your answers will be under oath – just as if you were testifying in court. You have to tell the truth. Do you understand? Do you have an attorney?"

I was a little shocked to find out that this was a deposition and not just an interrogation by the Sheriff's department. I had never heard of such a thing, except in civil matters like divorces and other law suits. Junior was sworn in and waived his right to an attorney. That seemed okay, because the questions didn't seem to treat him as a suspect. They were just getting information.

Junior admitted that he was standing over the body when the Sheriff and the rest of us got there, but Brody reminded them that the Medical Examiner had determined that Jonesy had been dead for at least an hour at that point. We learned that Jonesy was probably murdered before the tornado even happened. That was disturbing because it meant that he probably died as soon as he got home, just a few minutes after we talked to him at the diner. But it was good, because Junior was at Earl Rollins' place before the tornado.

But then the tone changed. One of the investigators or state lawyers pulled a large plastic bag out of his briefcase and set it on the table. It contained a small sledgehammer like the one we saw next to Jonesy's body. Alexandra Witherspoon continued:

"Mr. Carter, is this your hammer?"

"Nope."

"Have you seen it before?"

"Uh, nope…or, well, I've seen lots of 6-pound sledges like that one. But mine's pretty rusty and has an old beat up handle on it. That one looks pretty new – like the ones Ronnie sells at the hardware store."

"I see. Perhaps you bought a new one lately…from Ronnie. This one still has the price written in marker on the bottom of the handle."

Where was she going with this? I didn't like it. Junior shook his head.

"Nope."

She set her glasses down on the table and sat back in her chair, folding her arms as she nodded slowly. Then she leaned forward and pointed her pen right at Junior. "Can you tell me then, Mr. Carter, why your fingerprints are on this hammer, found at the scene – the same hammer which has been positively determined to be the hammer used to bash in the back of Mr. Jones' head and then to pound the stake through the chest of the victim?"

A small roar went up from the group inside the deposition room and in the hallway gallery where I was with Jake and the others. She was sounding very much like a prosecutor and not much at all like someone just gathering information.

"Don't answer that, Junior!" I hollered, banging on the glass, but he couldn't hear me.

Fortunately, he was too stunned to talk, and I rushed out of the viewing gallery, around the corner, and burst through the door to the interrogation room.

"This deposition is over!" I declared.

All faces turned toward me. I didn't even remember going into the room, but I was committed now. Ms. Witherspoon addressed me.

"Are you Mr. Carter's attorney, Miss?"

"I am not."

"Then…"

"Junior, tell them right now that you want a lawyer before you say another word."

The room was silent, as all eyes fell upon a confused Junior – except for his eyes, which were fixed on me. I nodded for him to do what I had asked.

"I want a lawyer before I say another word," he said, without taking his eyes off me.

I walked over to Junior. "Is he under arrest?" I asked the stunned lawyers and investigators. Only Brody was smiling, but he was trying hard to hide it.

"Well, we haven't…"

"Good. Junior, let's go! This whole state-run deposition lynch mob ambush is highly irregular in a criminal case to begin with, especially at this point. Sheriff, whose case is this anyway? Yours or the state's? Come on, Junior, let's get you out of this place."

He got up eagerly and with an exhale of relief. "Can I still get breakfast at the diner, Mercy?"

That remark probably didn't increase my status in the minds of the sophisticated state lawyers, but I didn't care. I was mad, as we stopped to the doorway. "Damn right you can, Junior. I'll make sure that Smoke has an Old School Hero Omelet waiting for you when we get back!"

"With pancakes?"

"With pancakes!"

Chapter Thirteen

The East End Shopping Center was the closest thing we had to a strip mall in Paint Creek. Originally, it was just the Shell Station on the corner by the edge of town, but Arnie Coulson bought the adjacent lots when they started to develop the big hill nearby around the time I was born. That's where I live now. He refurbished the old movie theater and added a few more storefronts, including Liz's Hair Salon and Jonesy's Butcher Shop. Ronnie Towns moved his hardware store out here last year too, I suppose since this is where most of the construction and renovation goes on these day. Plus, *Towns' End Hardware* has a nice ring to it – and I'm sure Arnie made him an offer he couldn't refuse.

It was a sunny afternoon, so I said goodbye to Grace and Wizard and walked down to Arnie's to check on my vintage Mercedes. My Dad had always dreamed of owning a Mercedes, and wanted that to be my name. But Mom was not going to allow her little girl to be named after a car. She wanted something more spiritual like Faith or Hope or Joy. Well, they finally compromised and named me Mercy. I'm happy with it.

Arnie was under a car as usual. It was splattered with dirt, and the tires were caked with mud and grass. Probably from the storm. I stopped outside the big open garage door and called Arnie's name.

"Not yet, Mercy," Arnie said, pushing himself out from under a blue-green sedan. "Had to order the axel from Germany. You're lucky they went into the business of refurbishing their classic cars over there. You'd never find parts for it at a junkyard – least ways, not around here."

"Arnie, it's been a week or more. What's the hold up?"

He stood up and grabbed a dirty shop towel to wipe off his greasy hands. "Well, that's what you get for buying that 1957 Mercedes, Merse."

I looked across the lot at my 1957 300-SL Roadster convertible. The polished metallic silver blue paint job made it glimmer as waves of late-day heat rose off the hood and trunk. I loved that car.

"Well, I guess when I bought the Old School Diner, I decided to go old school all the way, Arnie. And why did you order an axle?" I hadn't heard him mention an axle before. "I thought you said it was a U-joint or something like that."

"Well, I didn't want to worry you…"

Yeah, 'cuz I know what a U-joint is.

"…but that front axle developed a stress fracture – and you need a U-joint too. You gotta slow down over those speed bumps at the bottom of the hill, young lady. Good thing you got it to me when you did. It would've messed up a lot of stuff if it had broken clean through while you were moving."

How does he know about stress fractures? That's a

medical term. Maybe it's a mechanical term too.

"So, you got any idea when you'll get the parts?"

He stepped outside, stood next me, and spit. Fortunately, he aimed it downwind. Then he shook his head. "Won't be today."

Thanks for being so specific. "Okay. Stop in for lunch sometime. Haven't seen you at the diner for a while."

He nodded. "Been baggin' it lately, Mercy. Busy. You know how it is. When I get done changing the oil on the Pastor's car here, I got a brake job to do for Sam and Ethyl and then put on a set of new tires for Charlene." He smiled broadly.

Selling a set of tires would make it a really good day for Arnie, I supposed. "Ya, it never ends. So why don't you put the car up on the hoist to change the oil, Arnie? Seems like it would be easier."

"Easier? Naw. I just built this little ramp to get the front end of the car up a bit so I can get in there on my rolling rack. This way I can lay down while I work."

He had just enough of a smirk so I couldn't tell if he was pulling my leg or just savoring the tire sale. "Well, I'm going to say hello to Liz at the salon. Stop in soon, Arnie. Smoke is making his split pea soup tomorrow, and I'll have Deloris make her apple-cherry crisp." That should get him in there.

The row of stores was set back off the street to make room for parking in front. Jonesy's car was usually in front of the butcher shop, but there was no car there today. The horrible event was still burned into my mind's eye, and I said a little prayer for my friend, Carl aka Jonesy.

There was one of those little red Smart Cars in the corner of the lot, which I had seen around town a few times. *I wonder who that belongs to... That would be great for running errands around town.*

Junior's little green SUV was parked in front of Liz's salon down on the end, which struck me as a little odd, but I decided to poke my head into Ronnie's. I'd been meaning to pick up a new latch for the hamster cage before it cut my finger off or before my babies escaped.

"Hey! If it isn't the prettiest lady in McLean County! What brings you in today, Mercy?"

Ronnie was always a flatterer – and I loved it. I should hire him to be the voice in my "Mirror, Mirror on the Wall."

"Just need to fix the latch on my hamster cage, Ronnie."

He held up a finger, indicating that I should wait a minute, and ran off to one of the aisles to get it for me.

"I'm just going to snoop around for a while, Ronnie," I hollered to him.

I walked past some saws and wrenches and

screwdrivers, and then stopped to look at a pink plastic tool box with a few of the basics in it. *I should pick this up for the diner…or maybe for the house,* I thought. I took it by the handle and sashayed down the aisle. Then I stopped as something caught my eye, just as Ronnie walked up to me with several latches in hand.

"Tell me which one you like, Mercy, and I'll run up and put it on after I close up."

"One that's easy for me to get in, hard for them to get out…and looks cute! Say, Ronnie…" I reached into the bin on the shelf next to me and pulled out a small sledgehammer. "…have you sold any of these lately?" I looked on the end of the handle, and saw "8.99" written in black marker.

He looked in the bin and saw four more of the hammers. "Nope…but what the heck…I ordered a half-dozen of them a few weeks ago, so there should be six of them in there." I handed him the one I was holding, and he put it back with the others. "But there's only five of them here now. I wonder…"

He paused. He had a very concerned look on his usually happy face.

"What is it, Ronnie?" He shook his head and turned to walk back to the counter, but I had to know what had been such a cause of concern for him. I mean, if we find out who has the 6th sledgehammer, maybe we will know who the real killer is. It wasn't easy to get him to talk, but he finally opened up.

"Well, I guess there's no one else in the store right now, Mercy, but this is not something that can end up in the Paint Creek gossip mill."

He was right about that. I kept my eyes on his and just nodded my honest agreement.

"Well…" He leaned across the counter toward me and looked toward the door to make sure no one was coming. An old Ford pickup truck was just coming into the parking lot. "…the morning of the storm, it was kind of busy in here…a lot of people getting nails and duct tape and batteries and candles – supplies for the storm, I guess. I mean, Liz was here, Jonesy stopped in when he left the butcher shop, Hattie and Sandy stopped in, Vonnie bought some light bulbs while she waited for the reverend to fill up his gas tank and wash the car on the corner, and Pete Jenkins bought one of these disposable lighters and some chewing gum and said he was heading for the diner."

"So, what about Junior?"

"Well, anyway, I walked down the tool aisle there, and there was Junior, tossing one of those little sledges up and catching it after it made a spin. He kept on flipping it while I told him that he should probably start thinking about getting somewhere safe before the storm gets here. But when he got to the counter, her just bought a roll of coaxial cable, a wire cutter and crimper, and some connectors and wall plates. And, come to think of it, he paid with cash instead of putting it on his dad's company account."

Well, that could explain how Junior's prints got on the hammer. "But, he didn't have the hammer with him when he checked out, Ronnie?"

"Well, I know he didn't buy one. You don't think he would have stuck the handle under his belt and hung his untucked shirt over it, do you, Merse?"

The thought gave me a chill. "I've never known Junior to be a thief, Ronnie. His business is doing well." *And he already has an old beat up hammer just like it.*

"I've never had reason to suspect him of anything like that either, Mercy…but how did that other hammer disappear then?"

That was a good question, and made me wonder, just a little, if Junior really could be the killer. That would have to be the end of our conversation for now, as Earl Rollins came in the door.

"Afternoon, Earl," Ronnie greeted him. "What can I get you today?"

"Ahhh, just a quart of paint and some eight-penny nails to fix up the floor in my loft."

"Hi, Earl," I said. "I thought Jake and Junior were fixing up that loft for you. Was Junior's bid too high?"

"Oh, well, Junior was going to come out there the other day to give me a bid, but then that storm came up and he never got out there. It's for the best, I think. My back is feeling better now, and I'm just going to do it myself."

What? Junior's alibi for the time of Jonesy's death was that he was at Earl's. It's also his only reason for being out in that neck of the woods. I was sure that Brody must have followed up on Junior's story by now. I sent him a text and asked him when he would be back at the diner.

This was just great…Junior's fingerprints were on the murder weapon, he was seen holding it in the hardware store, and he lied about being at Earl's before the tornado struck. I just can't believe it. He replied in less than a minute:

Not sure, but I'll be at the City Council meeting tonight. Red's big library throw-down!

"Thanks, Ronnie! Can you just drop that lovely pink toolbox at my house tonight too? Side door is open. I'm going to try to catch a ride to the diner with Junior before he leaves. How much do I owe you? And don't let my babies get loose!"

"How about Sunday dinner at the diner, Mercy? That should cover it."

"Are you sure? That toolbox is $20."

Ronnie smiled and whispered to me, "You don't know what I paid for them at the warehouse…overstock! I'll bring you one for the diner too."

Chapter Fourteen

The East End Shopping Center was the closest thing
we had to a strip mall in Paint Creek. I thought the
afternoon had gotten just about as strange as it could get,
but the East End Shopping Center had more surprises in
store for me today. The door to the butcher shop was
wide open when I passed it on my way to Liz's parlor,
so I poked my head inside. I was surprised to see Pastor
D'Arnaud behind the empty meat case looking over
some paperwork on his clipboard.

"Pastor!" I guess I surprised him too because his
clipboard nearly hit the ceiling, and his reading glasses
flew off his stunned face.

"Uh…Miss Howard…so nice to see you," He said as
he picked up his pad and his eyeglasses. "Sorry. I was
engrossed in my numbers and wasn't expecting anyone
to come in today."

"Well, I'm sorry that I startled you. I guess I was a
little surprised to see you here in Jonesy's shop too. I
didn't mean to shriek at you. Are you…why…what
brings you…?"

He smiled and showed the kind eyes of his that I
hadn't seen for a while. "I thought you knew, Miss
Howard. I mean, you were one of our biggest customers.
Carl and I were partners here. I was just taking an
inventory of the meat we have left here."

"Oh! That's why you said you were going to the

butcher shop after the memorial service for Carl."

"Yes, Vonnie and I came here to put all the meat in the freezer until we could figure things out. Most of the fresh meat was actually in Jonesy's barn in the walk-in cooler there before everything was destroyed. He had a complete stainless-steel, UL-approved butcher shop there."

"Yes, he told me he had just gotten half a cow, or something. I was going to get a nice roast from him for Sunday dinner at the restaurant. But…"

"Yes. It's terrible. Terrible. I'm not sure what Vonnie and I will do with the shop yet, but you are welcome to stop in and take a look at what we have in the freezer. Perhaps we can both benefit from a transaction. Let's talk about it Sunday."

"Sure, Pastor."

I looked to make sure Junior's car was still there, and then headed over to Liz's hair salon. Junior was leaning very close to Liz at the counter. Was he whispering to her? Or kissing her on the cheek? I couldn't tell. Liz and Junior? She's a couple years older than me and ten years older than Junior, but you never know.

"Who's helping Babs out at the diner if you're here, Mercy?"

I recognized Deloris's throaty voice, and looked around the room. But where was she?

"Oh, for Pete's sake, Mercy. I'm right here."

"Oh! I didn't recognize you without your beehive, Deloris." She was in a chair, her hair down, with foil for the color and large coke-can rollers to get her ready for a new beehive.

"You know I come here every other Thursday. Don't look so surprised."

"Of course. Uh…It was really slow so I have Zack helping out behind the counter. Smoke has the kitchen handled. I just needed an afternoon to…"

"…to hang out with me for a change. Right. I suppose there'll be coffee grounds from here to kingdom come behind my counter when I get back there for dinner. That boy can cook, but he doesn't know how to clean."

I was going to defend Zack, but I knew she was right. "I'll make sure it's clean when you get back, Deloris."

I said hello to Vonnie, but she was reading a magazine under the hair dryer and didn't hear me. *Three birds with one stone,* I thought: *oil change, inventory, and hairdo. Smart.* I don't know how she can wear those white church gloves all the time. I wondered if it was a religious thing or a fashion thing – or if maybe she's a germaphobe. I've never seen her without them, but they seemed like they were getting longer and longer. Lately they almost reached her elbows. But they looked nice, I guess.

Liz was kind of staring at me as Junior headed for the door, and then she picked up the phone. "Junior!" I stuck out my thumb like a hitchhiker. "Can I catch a ride with you?"

I could see the gears turning in his brain. I was sure he was going to try to beat me out of a hamburger for driving services rendered, but he surprised me.

"Sure, Mercy. Let's go."

I wasn't getting any "killer" vibe from Junior as we rode the few blocks to the diner, but I still wasn't going to confront him with the new information I had learned about the hammer and his alibi. I had my little "equalizer" in my purse – just a .22 caliber Beretta pistol that my dad insisted I carry when I moved to the city. I'm a country girl and have always been comfortable around guns, but I didn't want a 9mm or a .38. I figured making a small hole in somebody would be enough to slow them down in a pinch. Besides, I can hit a beer can off a fence at 30 paces with my Beretta, so I can target a thigh or shoulder as the circumstances may require.

"So, were you making an appointment for a haircut with Liz, Junior? I thought you went to Wally's Barber Shop for your buzz cut."

"Ya, all the guys go to Wally's. I just wanted to talk to Liz."

Hmm. "I didn't know you and Liz had any…common interests."

"Well…ya…maybe not."

"So, why…"

Junior stopped at one of the two stop signs in town and looked at me. "Well, you know, Mercy…Liz knows stuff."

Now things were making sense. The hairdresser always hears all the gossip, and Liz is the queen of gossip in Paint Creek. "You should ask her out sometime, Junior. It looked like she likes you."

Junior's head jerked to attention. "Ya think so? I never thought about that. But there really aren't many women my age in town. She is kind of pretty and nice."

"So what did you learn from her, Junior?" I had to know.

He squirmed a little. "I'm not supposed to tell anybody."

"Come on…we're friends. There's a chocolate milkshake in it for you."

That was all it took. "Well, I was just trying to find out if she knew where Josie was. I figure the wife is always a prime suspect, especially since Josie disappeared pretty quick after Jonesy was killed – and I don't want to be charged with murder. That lawyer lady at the desperation got me a little scared, so I'm trying to solve this murder. Anyway, she said Josie called this morning to confirm her hair appointment for tomorrow."

I guess he meant the lady at the *deposition*. "But, I thought you said it was vampire hunters who killed Jonesy…"

"Well, she could be the vampire slayer too, like Buffy. I heard Josie was a gymnast in high school. But most vampire killers are either lawmen or holy men, so the Sheriff and the Pastor are still suspects in my book too, Mercy. Hey! It looks like Pops is here. I guess I'll come in for a while too. A milkshake would be good right now."

"Hold on a second, Junior. I know Liz – what did you give her in return for the information about Josie?"

He skillfully parallel parked his Rav4 behind his dad's truck in front of the diner and his face got bright red. "Um…nothing…you know…nothing."

That was way too suspicious for me to let it go. "No way, Junior. Liz always gets something in return. Spill."

He turned off the car and opened his door. "Well, I might have mentioned that you and Sheriff Hayes have been getting kind of cozy lately. That's all." He jumped out of the door.

"Junior! How could you?" That's why Liz was looking at me while Junior was whispering to her, and that's probably why she made a phone call when we were on our way out of the door. Great. By now the gossip mill will either have me engaged or pregnant, especially if she called Hattie Harper.

Of course, Hattie was in the diner with Sandy, her cell phone in front of her on the table. After giving me a smug, evil glare as I came through the door, she turned to Sandy and said loudly enough for all to hear, "I see they're having a sale on maternity wedding gowns at Yvette's Bridal Shop in Calhoun. I'm sure all the hussies and harlots in the area will be going there soon."

Wonderful – I'm engaged *and* pregnant – and a harlot.

My fight or flight instinct kicked in, and I chose to fight. I took three steps toward Hattie's table as Babs grabbed my arm and tried to pull me away, but I stood firm. "I don't know what you think you know, Hattie Harper, but how I live my life is none of your business. And there's nothing going on between me and the Sheriff."

"Mmhm. I know what happens to pretty young professional girls like you, once they've been to the city. All their morals fall away and they become obsessed with carnal pleasures. I could tell from the minute you walked into church with him for Jonesy's memorial service that you two were carrying on like a couple of feral rabbits. It was obvious he'd spent the night in your bed. Why else would you be arriving at church with him in the morning?"

"Because I asked him to pick her up for me!" Babs exclaimed loudly. "Now just mind your own business, you old busybody!"

"Hmmph."

This time I let Babs walk me to the counter, though I was still shaking with overflowing energy. Smoke was standing in the kitchen doorway, and Jake had gotten up from his stool too. They were staring down Hattie, but it was Red who settled the score:

"Your flying monkeys are calling you, Elvira. You better go home and feed them some of those scabs and maggots you scrape off your soul at night."

Chapter Fifteen

The council chamber was too small to hold all the people who wanted to weigh in on the debate over the new library. The old library was right across the street from the city offices. The second-floor event center of the Paint Creek Village Hall had been set up with a long head table and several rows of folding chairs. There was a stage behind them that was sometimes used for summer stock theater and, of course, Saturday afternoon Bingo.

I sat down next to Red, who had finagled a seat next to Deloris in the third row. "Hey there, Mercy! Ya know, we sure did have some groovy sock hops up here back in the day," he said with a chuckle. "I suppose you did too, huh?"

"Well, we didn't call them 'sock hops' in my day, Red," I said as I took my seat, "but we did have our Friday night dances here. Jake and Ronnie used to have a pretty good band that played here most weekends. And we are all very grateful to your generation for inventing

Rock 'n' Roll, or I'd probably still be trying to learn how to do the Cha Cha. Ready for your big moment in front of the crowd?"

"I sure am," he said with a wink.

"Got room for one more?" It was Brody, and he sat down next to me before I could answer him.

Of course, Hattie and Sandy were watching from across the aisle, so I made a show of whispering to him by pulling his head close to me. I think I surprised Brody a little bit too. "I've got some things to talk to you about, Brody," I whispered. I was eager to tell him what I had learned from Ronnie about the hammer and from Earl about Junior's alibi. Not that I wanted to get Junior in trouble, but it seemed like it was probably really important to the investigation.

"That's good, because I need to kick some ideas around with you too, Mercy. I need my 'Watson' to help me figure this out."

"Okay, Sherlock." I'm pretty sure that I'm the "Sherlock" in this crime-fighting duo, but I didn't want to bruise his male ego.

The mayor and Civil Defense Director, Bud Finster, led us in the Pledge of Allegiance and brought the meeting to order. The first order of business was to renew the contract with the Sheriff's department to provide law enforcement for Paint Creek. We suspended our police department when Chief Buttner died a few years back, and the county agreed to add an extra deputy to keep the town safe for a monthly fee. Stan had been the town cop with Ed Buttner, but he's been reporting to the County Sheriff ever since. That passed unanimously, and then they went on to set the budget and personnel to run the town's diner at the county fair in August. Sheriff Hayes was kind enough to nominate me to be in charge of the menu and the schedule. I guess that's what I get for showing up at a town council meeting.

"We'll now hear arguments for and against replacing the old Creekview Library with the new Robert C. Pattaway Media Center. The chair recognizes the Honorable William Robinson."

There was an easel with some architectural drawings of the proposed structure in front of the room as a man in a suit walked up to the microphone.

"Hey, Mercy, isn't that your old boyfriend?" Red asked.

I gave him a curious look and then looked back at the speaker. As soon as I heard his voice I realized it was Billy Robinson, the boy I went to Prom with a decade and a half ago. It turned out he was going to run to replace the retiring Congressman Pattaway next Fall, and it was mostly a campaign speech with lofty language about progress and the future. His pretty young wife and two perfect kids were the only ones who did much clapping. He gave me a little nod and salute as he headed back to his seat.

Then it was Red's turn to give his rebuttal. He inhaled some oxygen from his tank a couple of times and then set it aside as he stood up. The crowd gave him a standing ovation with plenty of cheers and whistles as he stepped to the front.

The crowd settled down a little as he approached the mic. "Most of us have spent our whole lives here in Paint Creek," he began. "Pete, Ed, Francine – and all the rest of you out there, well, we've know each other all our lives. Babs, Liz – I'm you're godfather. Mercy, I held you in my arms when you were only one day old, and I reckon that someday I'll be the one to walk you down the aisle."

That was sweet of him to say, and it would be true if there were an aisle in my future...which there's not. Of course, it did get a subtle guffaw from Hattie.

He continued: "And you council members and Bud at the head table here, you're all just regular folks like the rest of us. Well, Charlie, you might have a few more nickels than most of us from your feed business; and Agnes, you've done pretty well with your law practice doing up all of our contracts and things, but none of us are Rockefellers. And we're all real good friends. We're all at every wedding in town, we put on the Fourth of July parade together, we see each other at the Creekside, we're at all the town picnics and graduation parties together. Well...we're a big family.

"Now, I believe in progress as much as the next guy. But progress for the sake of progress, well...all it does is tear down tradition and eats away at all the things that hold us together. The town is the same size it was 75 years ago when that beautiful old library was built. Our parents and grandparents built it. We all studied there as students, and it holds special memories for all of us. The new plan even calls for them to get rid of that old crabapple tree behind the library."

That got a wave of disgruntled moans running through the crowd. The townsfolk became completely silent again as Red continued, his remarks really seeming to hit home for most people on an emotional level. I think that Billy Robinson was really surprised that everybody wasn't excited about a new library for the town.

Red said that a fancy new library in the middle of Paint Creek would be like a fancy crystal chandelier in the Old School Diner. That got a chuckle from the crowd, including me. Red's folksy style had a way of putting everything in perspective.

But Billy Robinson did not want to be outdone. He gauged the sentiment of the room quite well, like a skillful politician, and suggested that we don't let the federal money go to waste and that we still find a way to honor the outgoing Congressman. He recommended that the council should vote to add a media center in the lower level of the old library, as Red had suggested, and build a new bridge over Paint Creek.

He also thought it would be a good idea to name the bridge and the street that crossed the bridge and passed between the Village Hall and the library after Congressman Pattaway, who was born in our town. Maybe he would be a good representative in Congress. Nobody really minded losing the much-mocked name, "DeRange Avenue." It was time to get rid of some of our Confederate memories anyway. Even though Kentucky was officially a neutral border state in the Civil War, we still had plenty of secessionist-sympathizing politicians after the war. We'll see what happens, but it seemed that the teardown of the old library was off the table.

Chapter Sixteen

A dozen or so of us pulled some chairs in a circle and gathered in the back of the meeting hall to have a little reception for Red. I could see he was a little pale after his triumphant speech, so I insisted that he put on his oxygen tubes. He didn't like using it in front of people, but he agreed – which meant that he really needed it. Of course, the conversation quickly turned to Jonesy's murder.

"You got this thing solved yet, Sheriff?" Jake Senior asked. "I don't like people thinking that my boy here had anything to do with it, so you gotta find out who did."

Brody turned to me with a concerned look. "I might have to arrest Junior in the morning, Mercy," He whispered to me, and then smiled at Jake and nodded. He had already checked out Junior's alibi, and I told him during the council meeting about Junior flipping the hammer at the hardware store the morning before the storm hit.

Earl Rollins was there and spoke up. "I been hearing that you've been using me as your cover story, Junior. But truth is, like I told you, Sheriff, Junior wasn't at my place before the tornado hit. Makes him look pretty guilty, telling lies like that, if you ask me."

Jake was outraged, and stood up to defend his son's honor. "Junior is no liar, Earl. If anyone's a liar, it's you!"

Junior turned pale and had a sheepish look on his face as his dad continued to defend him. "Pops…" he said softly, but Jake didn't hear him.

Other people had been gathering in small groups before leaving, just to greet their friends and be neighborly, and they were soon attracted by the loud commotion coming from our circle. Sandy Skitter looked toward the ladies' room to see if Hattie was returning yet, and then walked over toward our group.

"Junior, just go ahead and tell them," she told him, leaning over his shoulder.

He looked at her and then mustered up all of his courage and stood up. "Pops," he said again. "Pops!" He finally got Jake's attention.

Everybody was silent and looked at Jake. I thought my heart was going to pound right through my chest. What was Junior going to say? Then Junior burst into tears and fell to his knees.

"I'm guilty, Sheriff! Put the cuffs on me, and throw me in jail!"

His sobs echoed through the now-silent room. *My gosh, could this be real?*

Sandy looked bewildered. "Junior! You couldn't have done it. You were with me and Hattie the whole time during the storm. You didn't leave Hattie's house until the minute the siren stopped sounding."

What was Junior doing at Hattie's house?

"I know!" Junior continued sobbing and he spoke. "I did it…I went over to Hattie's when I left the hardware store, and…" He stopped and looked around, but didn't continue.

"Tell them, Junior!" Sandy urged. "Tell them!" But Junior was too distraught to speak, so Sandy spilled the beans. "He hooked Hattie's house up to the cable TV line in back of her house. He didn't kill Jonesy, he was just helping Hattie steal cable service."

"I know it's wrong to steal cable, Sheriff," Junior blubbered, "but I did it anyway. Miss Hattie gave me twenty bucks to do it, plus she gave me twenty bucks at the hardware store too to buy the cable and connectors and said I could keep the change from that too. I'm a bad man, Sheriff Hayes. I'm sorry!"

"So, what were you doing out at Jonesy's when he was killed?" the Sheriff asked, pointedly.

Junior started to get control of himself and stood up. "I…I was heading out to Earl's then, after I got the cable all hooked up, but I never made it. I saw that the twister had already destroyed the barn, so I pulled into Jonesy's driveway to check on him, but I couldn't get all the way in because of the downed trees. I waited in the car until the rain let up. That's when I walked over toward the house and found Jonesy laying there, dead."

Hattie Harper strutted up, and all eyes turned to her. She looked at Sandy with accusing eyes.

"What did you do, Sandy Skitter? You were sworn to

secrecy forever. Hmmph." She turned abruptly, with her nose in the air and started to walk out.

"But, Hattie!" Now Sandy was distraught. Her whole life was built around her association with Hattie. "You can't let Junior get charged with murder just so you can have free cable!"

Hattie stopped and turned. "Why not? He's just a useless slob anyway, just like his daddy…always talking about space aliens and weather machines. Hmmph. They should both be locked up anyway, away from decent people. Besides, I can do anything I want. This is my town, and everybody knows it." She walked out, and I went to comfort Sandy. Babs and Jake were tending to Junior.

Smoke and Deloris stood up and came toward me. "Mercy," Smoke said, "I think we have to call an emergency session of 'late night diner.' These people have a lot to gossip about, and they're going to throw us out of here in a few minutes."

"Great idea," I agreed. "Just coffee and pastries should be good. We still have three or four fresh pies and some cobbler. There should be plenty of ice cream."

"I'll turn on half the griddle for hamburgers too," he said.

"And I'll make some coffee and iced tea," Deloris added.

Smoke made the announcement to the crowd, and most

of the lingerers followed them out the door.

Bud was starting to turn out the lights. "The chief's office is still available to you on the first floor, Sheriff Hayes. It's included in your contract with us, you know. You two can move down there if you've got more…police business to discuss."

He winked at Brody, and I rolled my eyes. Nobody loves and respects women more than older guys, but nobody can be bigger chauvinists either. I'll chalk it up to generational differences for now.

"We'll take our conversation downstairs, Mayor. Thanks."

Chapter Seventeen

The setting moon cast hazy shadows over the desk in the first-floor office. It was quite spartan with just a wooden desk, a file cabinet, a fax machine, a green banker's lamp, and a chair on each side of the desk. Brody stood at the window, looking out at the night sky with his hands clasped behind his back, and I leaned on the tall file cabinet next to him.

"So, it looks like Junior isn't your man, Sheriff. What now?"

He sighed but kept his gaze on the stars. "Well, I'm very relieved that Junior can be ruled out now – if his story is true."

"Oh, it's true. Ronnie Towns told me Junior was in his store buying cable and supplies the morning of the murder, and Hattie was there too – and he paid cash, just like he said. Did you find Jonesy's wife yet?"

He sat on the corner of the desk and looked at me blankly. "Nobody's seen hide nor hair of her since the evening of the murder, when Florence left the farm house after dinner. Josie told Florence her sister was coming that evening to stay with her, but it turns out she doesn't have a sister. Her mother in Indiana hasn't seen her either. But her car is still there, parked behind the farmhouse right where Jonesy left it. She didn't buy a bus ticket either."

"Oh, my gosh! That scares me, Brody. I hope she's okay."

"Well, there's no reason to think there's been any foul play. And, well…it kind of puts her on the top of my suspect list now."

"What about the butcher shop?"

He looked confused. "What about it?"

"Well, I mean, maybe there could have been some kind of business motive. The Pastor was Jonesy's business partner…not that he had anything to do with it, but maybe there could be a money trail that points somewhere."

"The state team already checked it out. The books are clean as a whistle…just small cash withdrawals for salaries."

It seemed that Brody had done a pretty thorough job on the investigation. "So, the state's lawyers are still running things?"

Brody smiled. "It seems a beautiful young nurse and restaurateur scared them off. The odd circumstances with the stake through his heart has kept the media circus going strong throughout the state, so they do want to get this thing solved. I have to check in with Alexandra Witherspoon every couple of days."

A twinge of jealousy ran through my stomach. "That must be awful for you, having to talk to that gorgeous blonde runway model so often." *Did I say that out loud?*

One corner of Brody's lip curled with the first smile I'd seen on him since the meeting upstairs ended. He stood up and folded his arms. "Don't tell me the indomitable Miss Howard is…jealous?"

I turned a little bit away from him and tried to hide my pout. "Don't be silly. Why should I be jealous of a tall, shapely, brilliant, successful, hideous beast like her?" My gosh, I was turning into an insecure high school girl.

Brody stepped closer, lifted my chin with his strong finger, and tilted my head towards him. His face was a little too close, and the intimacy made me inhale quickly and deeply. "You shouldn't be. That hideous beast can't hold a candle to you, Mercy."

He smiled as our eyes were fixed on each other for a brief eternity. I would have gladly accepted his kiss in that moment, but instead he just pulled me into a warm embrace and held my head against his shoulder. "You're the only shapely model I want walking my runway, Mercy Howard." Then he held both my shoulders at an arm's length. "And if you're a good girl and stop pouting, I'll buy you an ice cream cone tomorrow."

I punched him in the shoulder and tried to squelch a laugh. "Careful with the witty comments there, buster. I'm supposed to be the clever, snarky one in this…um…group." *Group? Now I'm a babbling idiot…and how did my eyes get moist?*

"I'm going to use the ladies' room, Brody. Be right back."

"Sure. I'll get some coffee from the vending machine. Double cream, no sugar for you?" he asked as he fumbled for change in his pockets.

How did he know how I took my coffee? I felt a little flattered that he paid enough attention to remember. "Yes, that's right." He was making frustrated grunts as he pulled a few pennies and nickels out of his pocket. I pointed to my purse on the desk. "Inside zipper pocket," I said. "There's probably enough change for a down payment on a 747 jetliner in there."

When I returned there were two coffee cups on the desk, but Brody had an odd look on his face.

"What is it, Brody? Is something wrong?"

He sat on the corner of the desk, and I took the chair by the door. "Mercy…you've got…a pistol in your purse. That's a dangerous weapon. Do you know how to use it? Do you have a permit to carry?"

And why would his assumption seem to be that I don't know what a gun is for and don't know how to handle it? "Yes, I have a little Saturday Night Special. I've had it for about 12 years or so, Brody, ever since I left Paint Creek for college in Louisville. And I'm sure I'd have no trouble polishing you off in a showdown on Main Street at High Noon." There was more than a tinge of competitive righteous indignation in my tone, but I was a little offended. I wished I hadn't said it in quite the way that I did, but I said it.

"Well…I didn't mean to imply…"

"Yes, you did." *Shut up, Mercy…*

"Say, Mercy, I'm going to the shooting range tomorrow for my bi-monthly practice. Why don't you come along? You can show me what you've got. We can do the regular target practice inside, and then we can try the Old West town they have set up in back with bad guys jumping out of doorways and stuff. Then I can update your permit when we're done. I'll buy you lunch if you can outshoot me."

I gave him the stink-eye and pushed the brim of my imaginary cowboy hat up a couple of inches. "Bring your wallet, cowboy. Loser buys lunch at the Hideaway Cove Country Club. I hope you like crow."

Chapter Eighteen

The Sheriff rolled up in front of the diner at exactly 9:00 a.m., and I went out to meet him. The breakfast rush was over, and my food order was emailed in.

"Good morning Sheriff!" I smiled brightly as he walked around the car to meet me on the sidewalk. His eyes were feasting on my body from head to toe, and it felt good.

"Morning, Mercy. I see you're ready for some outdoor action."

I was wearing my best skinny jeans, white athletic shoes that I had never worn outside, and what Deloris called a "peek-a-boo" scoop neck tank top. My hair was in a ponytail, and I put on just enough makeup to make my lips and eyes pop.

"Yup... but still presentable enough for our lunch at the Country Club, Brody." He nodded in agreement and opened the passenger door for me. "I see you brought your own car instead of your patrol car...that's good."

"Well, yeah, I didn't want the town gossips to think you were under arrest. But I still wore my uniform so they won't charge me at the shooting range."

I stepped up into the very high and over-sized SUV. I was glad I wasn't wearing heels and that my jeans had a little stretch to them. The tall lawman got in the driver's side and turned the key. The big engine hummed quietly and smoothly. It had the feel of luxury, especially compared to Jake's pick-up truck, which vibrated like an unbalanced washing machine in the spin cycle.

"Okay, Brody, let's figure out this murder. We should have all the evidence we need; we're just missing something when we try putting it all together." I put on my sunglasses and pulled down the car's sun visor, which had a mirror on it. I looked good, and Brody kept stealing glances as he made an illegal U-turn in front of the diner, almost clipping a parked car in front of Brandi's donut shop. I smirked and pretended not to notice as he blushed and headed for the shooting range, half-way between Paint Creek and Calhoun.

"Well, let's go over the evidence, Mercy. Maybe we can figure it out before lunch."

"Okay, well, what time did Jonesy…you know…die?"

"Coroner says between 1:00 and 2:00 in the afternoon. She couldn't narrow it down any more than that because the cold rain may have affected lividity and body temperature."

"Well, it shouldn't really affect postmortem lividity. That's just the blue patches on the skin from the blood settling. I did notice some early signs of *rigor mortis* in the eyelids and jaw and that could have been accelerated a little by cooler temperatures from the storm. What was the rectal temperature?"

He gave me a weird look and pointed toward the autopsy report on the console. I looked it over.

"Well, it says that the rectal temp was 89.5 degrees at 7:45 p.m. So, the Glaister equation would put the time of death at 1:45."

He gave me an odd look again.

"The body temperature drops about 1.5 degrees Farenheit every hour after death, so nine degrees would put the time of death 6 hours earlier, at 1:45. Since the air was cooler due to the storm, I think it would be more likely that he died earlier that that rather than later. He left the diner the same time the siren began to sound, and I remember looking at my watch. It was 1:20, so he must have been killed shortly after he got home."

Brody nodded. "The funnel cloud touched down at two o'clock according to Florence in the farmhouse next door, which jibes with the National Weather Service. It didn't pick up the whole barn like Junior told us before – he wasn't there yet – but it did completely destroy it in short order. Then it wandered off to the Northeast and dissipated."

"What time did the siren stop? That's when Junior left Hattie's, according to Sandy last night."

"Bud has it on a 30-minute timer. That way he can take cover, and the people have plenty of time to get the message too. So, it would have shut off ten minutes before the twister hit the barn, if your start time is right. Junior had to drive across town and then a few miles past the creek, so he probably got there right afterwards. His car was outside the fallen trees, so he arrived after the tornado passed through, but Jonesy's car was near the house. That means he got there before the tornado hit. The all-clear didn't start until about 2:30, when I came into the diner and you all came out of the basement."

"Yeah, we were down there for about an hour. I remember hearing it when we were coming up the stairs. Still no word from Josie?"

He shook his head.

"You know, I was talking to him before he left the diner that day, Brody. He wanted me to go out to the farm and talk to Josie. She had told him she wanted to talk to him about something, and he was really nervous about it. He thought she was going to tell him she wanted a divorce. I wonder…"

"That's not what she was going to tell him, Mercy."

I turned my head toward him quickly, curious about what he knew. "How do you know that, Brody?"

"Well, I interviewed Florence Carwinkle for almost an hour the day after the murder. She was the only one who really spent any time with Josie after we found the body."

"Yes, I remember, she stayed in the house there with her for the rest of the afternoon. So?"

"So, she told me what Josie was going to tell Carl that night."

He slowed down for the railroad tracks just outside of

town, but didn't say any more. From his smug look I knew that he was waiting for my female curiosity gene to make me beg him to tell me more.

"Oh. That's interesting." I smiled at him politely. "It looks like it's really going to be a lovely day, Brody. Why don't you drop me off by the side of the road right here. I think I'll pick blueberries in the woods today, and you can pick me up on your way back after your target practice – and after you've solved this case by yourself." I smiled politely again, trying to do my best impression of a Southern belle.

"Okay, okay. I'll tell you."

"Tell me what?"

"Right. Well, Josie told Florence that she felt terrible for spending so much time away from the house lately, and now she realized that Jonesy was everything she ever wanted. She wanted to apologize to him and reconcile. And now it was too late."

"Hmm. Interesting. So, if that's true, then she doesn't really have a motive for killing him. Did she tell Florence if she was having an affair?"

"She just told her that she had become bored with her life and felt like she needed more – midlife crisis stuff, I guess. So, maybe it was an affair or maybe she ran off and drove race cars for a little excitement a few nights a week. Hard to say."

We passed the Incarnation Church and pulled into the

parking lot in front of Tully's Shooting and Archery Range just a couple hundred feet further down the road.

"Oh! There's that little red Smart Car again. I have to find out who it belongs to so I can ask them how they like it. It seems so practical, and kind of cute too."

"That car? That belongs to Pastor D'Arnaud."

"Really? I thought he had a regular-sized car."

"I think he does, but his wife drives the other one. That's the only one I've ever seen him driving. The holy man must be practicing again. I see him out here fairly often, maybe because he lives practically next door."

"Huh."

Chapter Eighteen

"Hey, there, Mercy!" Tully greeted me when we checked in at the desk. "I haven't seen you out here for a while."

"Well, the Sheriff thinks I need some practice, Tully."

"Practice? Why, you earned your Sharpshooter badge when you were 12, Mercy, and became a High Master before you graduated high school. That's the black belt of marksmanship. The Sheriff here just became a Marksman-2 last month. He might make Sharpshooter again by fall if he keeps practicing."

Again?

Brody looked at me with his jaw open. "High Master?"

I shrugged. "Some girls twirled batons. I shot pistols and rifles."

Tully gave us the guest book and the standard waiver to sign. "I hope she didn't rope you into any big money bet before you got here Sheriff," he said with a wink at me.

Brody shook his head weakly. "Just lunch."

Tully chuckled and looked at me. "At the Hideaway?"

I nodded enthusiastically and licked my lips.

"I recommend the 12-ounce filet with sautéed

mushrooms and Béarnaise sauce, Mercy."

"Hey! This is just lunch, you guys!" Brody was getting worried.

I patted his chest with my hand. "Don't worry, cowboy. When I'm in blue jeans, I'm a burger girl – but when you see me in a red dress and four-inch heels, watch out. Let's go shoot."

"Are you going to use your little Beretta, Mercy, or do you want something a little more substantial for target practice?"

"I brought a 9 millimeter Glock for her, Tully," Brody said. "We'll see how she handles a real gun."

"Ha!" Tully scoffed. "You want the .357 or the .44 Magnum, Mercy?"

"I don't want to scare him, Tully. I'll go with the standard law enforcement Glock so we're on a level playing field today." Besides, Tully's *Dirty Harry* .44 Magnum Smith and Wesson kind of scared me. The last time I used it my wrist hurt for two weeks from the recoil.

"You two should come out here and take out your aggressions on each other with a little paint ball on the weekends. It's been real popular since we added it this spring. You can shoot each other all day long."

"That does sound delightful, Tully!" I looked at Brody with a devilish grin."

"We'll definitely do that, Tully," Brody said, "but today we're going to try our luck in Old Dodge City after we practice inside."

"Sounds good, but I thought you didn't like that course Sheriff…reminded you too much of kicking in doors in Afghanistan…"

Whoa!

"…There's a rack of vests by the back door – they're required, of course. The reverend is probably still out there. He likes to go through it quite a few times when he's here. Say, Mercy, do me a favor."

"Sure, Tully. What is it?"

"Holster up this paint ball gun and give it a try when you're done with the course. I got a fence back there at the end of the course lined up with whiskey bottles and beer cans. This is supposed to be pretty accurate at 10 yards or so, but I'd like your opinion before I order up a bunch of them. Some of the customers aren't happy with the ones I got now."

"Will do, Tully." I strapped on the belt and holstered the large CO_2 pistol. "Ready, Sheriff Hayes?"

"After you, High Master."

All of the evidence we had discussed on the way was rolling through my mind, and I was trying to make sense out of it as we shot the targets. I emptied my clip into the paper target 15 yards away.

"So, where do you suppose Josie is, Brody?" I asked as he slowly lined up a shot on the target, which was a black silhouette of a man's torso and head.

"I suppose someplace far away by now, Mercy. She must have left in a hurry. Didn't look like she packed anything, not even her toothbrush. She didn't even grab her sweater off the coat rack by the door." His hand seemed a little unsteady, and he kept aiming the whole time he was talking. Then he finally shot once.

"I think the bad guy would either be gone or would have a half-dozen rounds in your chest by now, Brody. This isn't precision rifle practice, it's self-defense and law enforcement quick response in here. You don't have anything to prove to me, Brody. Just plug a few shots in the bad guy – center of mass – before he gets away."

He shot seven more times quickly, and we hit the button to bring the targets to us on the zipline so we could see how we did.

"Too much coffee this morning, Brody? You seem a little jittery."

"Uh…yeah, yeah. I must've drunk a whole pot."

"Well, I don't know, Brody. I don't think Josie would run away without a word. I'm worried about her."

We looked at the targets. Mine had a tight cluster of four bullets in the head and four in the heart. Brody's had six spread out around the whole torso and two that missed to the left.

"Nice groupings," he said.

"Your guy is just as dead. Let's make it fair this time," I said as he attached a new paper target for each of us. "You bring yours in to 10 yards, and I'll move mine out to 25 yards. This one is for lunch." I could tell his manhood felt challenged, but we set our targets at those distances. "Five seconds to unload your clip from the time you pick up your gun. You go first."

He picked up his gun and put eight quick shots into the target. He had done pretty well and looked pleased with himself. "Your turn, ma'am."

My mind was still whirring over the evidence as I picked up the Glock, aimed, and pulled the trigger one time. Then I stopped as a revelation came into my mind. Brody looked confused as we brought our targets in. We looked at his first: three in the belly, three in the right shoulder, and two in the left shoulder.

"Looks like he's in for a few hours of surgery," he said. "I thought I'd done better than that. But, unless your one shot – at 75 feet – hit him right in the heart, you might be buying lunch today after all. Let's take a look…"

Brody took a look at the single bullet hole right between the eyes of the target image and just shook his head. "Nice work, Mercy."

I was still silent and had a faraway look in my eyes.

"What's wrong Mercy? Is everything all right."

"Brody," I looked at him with a serious and unblinking gaze, "I know who the killer is."

Chapter Nineteen

"So, am I going to have to go into the woods and pick blueberries, or are you going to tell me who killed Carl Jones, Mercy?"

I inhaled deeply and let it out with a sigh. "Let me just noodle it around for a while first, see if there are any flaws in my logic. We'll talk about it during lunch." I sent off a detailed text to Deloris at the diner, put the safety on the Glock, and tucked it under the holster belt. "Nice handgun, well-balanced and accurate. Are we going outside to shoot some outlaws?"

"Yep. Let's stop in the cantina – I'll treat you to a soda and a bag of chips."

"Trying to fill me up before lunch?"

He laughed. "That's not a bad idea!"

It was a nice break, and I began to see things in Brody's face and eyes that he had never shown me before. He didn't want to talk much about Afghanistan, but I got the feeling that he had been part of a special forces unit.

"Well, time's a-wasting!" I said, standing up. "That five-minute break turned into 20, but it was nice. The vests are over here."

We got suited up and went outside. The red light was on, indicating that another group was still on the course. A lovely teenaged girl was in a chair, monitoring the flow for Tully.

"You have to wait for the light to turn green," she said, "and then you have to stay together so you don't…"

"…shoot each other," I said with a smile as we sat on the bench.

She nodded. "Follow the green line through the course, it's kind of a maze, and be ready for things to pop out at you. There will be life-sized posters appearing quickly in doorways, around corners, and even in upstairs windows. Some will be criminals and some will be innocent bystanders – don't shoot them, or it will really hurt your score. Just two shots per target are allowed. That will get you through the course with three 8-round clips. One of you can take all the targets on the left and the other can take the ones on the right, or you can take them both and get a composite team score. How long it takes you to shoot once the target appears and how long it takes you to get through the course are just important to your score as accuracy. Any questions?"

"I think that covers it…Mandy. Great job!" I said, looking at her name tag. The name sounded familiar. "Are you Lurleen's daughter?"

"Yes, Miss Howard."

"My gosh, you were just starting school when I left town, and look at you now!"

The light turned green, and we wandered off toward our adventure 20 yards away.

"Team?" I suggested.

"That's fine."

Pastor D'Arnaud gave us a friendly wave as we crossed paths as he walked back into the waiting area.

I'm going to have to ask him about that Smart Car when we're done.

"Now tell me who killed Jonesy, Mercy." Brody said, almost whining. "You said you got it all figured out, so let me hear your theory."

There was a six-foot high wall of stone with steel rising another six feet above that to keep stray bullets from hitting the building. We walked around it to the starting point. There was a big sign with all the rules that Mandy had already told us, and a big industrial looking button to start the round. I pushed it.

"Let's move. Partner," Brody said, and led the way along the green line toward the first building in town. The sign on it said *General Store*. The front door popped open and poster of a lady pushing a baby carriage came out.

"I don't know – she looks pretty mean," I said. "Maybe we should shoot her."

Brody raised an eye brow at me but a gunslinger popped out from behind the corner of the store, and Brody shot him in the chest in a split second.

"Wow. Good reaction time, partner." I was impressed how quickly he reacted and took the accurate shot. But Brody was silent, and his eyes were focused. It was as if his instincts had taken over, and he was totally in the zone.

"It sounds like there's something going on in the blacksmith shop up ahead," he finally said.

His ears must be tuned in extremely well too, because I hadn't heard anything. "Maybe something's getting ready to pop," I said. "I'll check on it, so keep any shots to the left side of the street for the time being."

He nodded and took out a pair of bad guys by the saloon.

I poked my head inside the open front wall of the blacksmith shop, expecting to see a blacksmith or an outlaw. Instead, I got the surprise of a lifetime. I heard the click of an old-fashioned revolver being cocked and then a low quiet voice.

"Drop the gun, Mercy. Your life depends on it."

I hated to give up my weapon at the one moment when I might, for the first time in my life, actually need it. But I was no fool; I tossed it to the ground a few feet behind me. Then a shadowy figure began to emerge from behind the anvil. I knew who it was before I even saw him.

"Good morning Pastor D'Arnaud. I've been meaning to ask you about your Smart Car. It looks like it might be pretty economical for running around town."

"Cut the happy talk, and turn around."

"Yes, sir. You're the one making the rules right now."

"So, you think you know who killed Carl Jones?"

"Yes…in fact I'm almost certain of it."

"I suppose you think you're pretty smart. Now, very slowly, raise your hands, turn around, and walk out into the street."

I felt his gun in my back, and he nudged me forward. Brody was across the street in front of the saloon, and he quickly raised his gun when he saw me being held hostage. The Pastor put his left arm around my neck and put the barrel of his gun on my shoulder.

"Do you like my perfume, Pastor? It's called *Woman on Top*. Kind of ironic right now, I guess, since you clearly have the upper hand."

"Shut up. Tell your cowboy to disarm, or his pretty little girlfriend will get a bullet in her head."

"Brody! He wants you to throw down your gun."

"I can take the shot, Mercy." Brody hollered back from

20 feet away. "I can get him right in the forehead, no problem."

The Pastor nuzzled his head a little closer and halfway behind mine.

"I know you can, Brody. But there's no need to kill him."

"Drop it, Sheriff!" He ordered, "Or so help me, I'll kill her."

I could feel my captor shaking. "Don't drop it, Brody, but go ahead and lower your gun."

"But, Mercy…"

"Trust me, Brody."

He slowly lowered his gun and stood up straight.

"You're playing with your life, Mercy." The Pastor sounded distraught, and the tone of his voice sounded like he was begging me. I could feel the sweat on his face against the back of my neck. "I said I would kill you, now make him drop it."

"But you're not going to kill me, are you, Pastor?" I took his left hand in mine and pulled it gently away from my neck. "Because you're not a killer." I slowly turned halfway around so I could see both him and Brody. "You're not a killer, are you, Pastor?"

"Of course, I am. I killed Jonesy. Why else would I be doing this right now?"

"Because you're trying to protect somebody."

The Pastor jerked as a poster of a fat blacksmith lurched forward. I reached slowly for the barrel of his gun, pushing it lower. Then I took the gun and carefully released the cocking mechanism. I spun the revolving chamber and saw that there were no bullets in the gun. Then I heard some motion beyond the far corner of the saloon and saw a shadow of a woman jutting out towards me. She stepped out into the street with her pistol raised.

"You're not the killer, Pastor, because she is." I pointed to the gun-toting woman who had just joined us. It was Vonnie D'Arnaud, the Pastor's wife.

Chapter Nineteen

"There's no way you could know that I killed that son-of-a-bitch, Mercy," Vonnie said in an almost calm manner. "I had every detail covered perfectly."

Wow. This was not the same Vonnie I had known for several years. Her demeanor, her crude language – this was a whole different personality. She kept on talking.

"But he had it all coming, keeping Josie a prisoner in that marriage, just like I'm prisoner in mine." She took a few steps closer. She was still 30 feet away, but she was strolling a small step closer with every sentence or two. The sun would be up above the high roof of the two-story saloon and in my eyes in a few minutes.

Come on, Vonnie...a little bit closer...

Brody's eyes met mine. I knew what was on his mind, as he still had his Glock in his hand, but I shook my head and diverted my eyes downward toward my holster. Vonnie kept talking.

"Hey, you know, Kentucky is a death penalty state, so they can only kill me once. Which means I might as well kill all of you. So, I guess it won't hurt to tell you the whole story before you die."

"You see, Jonesy thought that Josie was sneaking out of the house to have an affair with my Donny..."

The Pastor's name was Donald D'Arnaud.

"…and Donny thought that I was sneaking out to play around with Jonesy. I guess they would see each other's cars coming and going at late hours." She laughed. "As if I would have anything to do with that horrible little man. Ha! It was me! Me, that Josie was interested in."

The Pastor looked stunned at this revelation.

"Oh, no, no…not in that kind of way. We both talked about having a fresh start, getting away from our ball-and-chains that were tying us down to this dull little town. It's like being in hospice care, waiting to die here. We went out to nightclubs and casinos, Josie and I, where real men paid attention to us. We were going to run away – maybe Memphis or St. Louis – and start our own business. Maybe a nice little bistro – not a dump like yours, Mercy, full of old trolls from under a bridge…"

Well, thank you very much, Vonnie.

"…but a nice place with nice people – you know, in polite society. But then she called the whole thing off…said we were being foolish, and she wanted to stay with that…that…butcher."

I could see the anger rising in her veins as she continued. "So, last Thursday morning Donny and I were in the hardware store. Everybody was talking about the big storm, and I saw Junior in there whispering to Hattie. I knew I couldn't shoot Jonesy because they could trace the bullet back to my gun. I thought about framing Donny – everybody suspected he was having an affair with Josie anyway, so he'd have a good reason to kill Jonesy so he could have her all to himself."

I didn't suspect they were having an affair…

"So, I saw Junior walking up and down the aisles. I set one of those big hammers on the floor in the middle of the aisle just before he got to the tool aisle so he would pick it up and get his fingerprints all over it. I was always wearing my white gloves, so my prints wouldn't get on it, you know. Of course, the fat fool took the bait. He picked it up and started playing with it, and then put in on top of the others. I just dropped it into my purse and walked out with it. Donny wanted to take me to breakfast at the diner, but I told him just to drop me off at home. I guess he went by himself, and I took my car out to Josie's place and parked in the trees, out of sight. The rest was easy."

"Tell us how you did it, Vonnie," I asked. "I'm curious how you got that stake through his chest."

"Oh, it was easy, Mercy! I called Josie, so I knew she had asked Carl to come home. I waited for him by the barn. He sent Josie into the storm cellar and came to secure the barn door. He used a crowbar to pull off the old board that had been holding the door closed, and that piece splintered off and fell to the ground. I surprised him when I went up to confront him, and he told me to get into the storm cellar. Ha! I started to beat on his chest with my fists, and he grabbed my arms real tight and pushed me away. You can still see the bruises…the beast."

That's why she was wearing long gloves lately…

"Well, he turned around to walk away, and I took the hammer out of my purse and smacked him in the back of the head." She giggled a little. "He went down like a brick! Well, I was feeling pretty great, of course, but I wanted to make sure he was dead. So, I saw that piece of wood and used the hammer to pound it right through his heart. Pretty clever, don't you think?" Then she laughed out loud. "Oh, it was so rich when I heard about Junior's vampire story. Ha ha! I figured that would just make him look even more guilty, trying to shift the blame to a vampire killer! Well, then, of course, I went back to my car. My, God, that tornado was so scary! Thank goodness it went off in the other direction. Then I drove off, and you guys were too busy playing crime-fighter to even notice."

Nope. I noticed.

"It's all right, sweetheart!" the pastor hollered to his murderous wife. "It will be okay! We'll move to St. Louis and open the business of your dreams!"

He was a slobbering mess, poor man. But the sun's glow was starting to appear over the top of the saloon. I knew how far away a seven-yard target looked, and I figured she was not much further than that right now. I didn't trust the accuracy of a paint ball gun outside of 25 feet, but Tully said this was a good one. I hoped he was right.

"Just put the gun down, honey," the Pastor begged her, trying to sound calm and rational.

It was good that he was talking to her, but it did bring her eyes too close for me to make a move. Then I got my chance. A gust of wind came up and blew her hair into her face. As she put her hand in front of her eyes to brush it back I pulled the paint gun from the holster, aimed for a full second, and then shot. Splat! The ball hit her forehead with the force of a punch from a boxing glove and knocked her out. She fell straight backwards, her gun hand limp at her side.

"No! Noooooo!" The Pastor ran towards his wife, red paint streaming down her face and into her eyes. "Why? Why did you have to do that, Mercy? Why?!"

I knelt beside her next to him and wiped the paint off with my hand. "Pastor, it's all right – paint. It's just a paintball." I put my arm around his shoulder, and he just crumbled and wept.

"It's okay, sweetheart," he whispered to his obviously disturbed wife. "We're going to get you some help. It's okay…everything's okay." She began to rouse and sat up.

Brody was standing over us now with his handcuffs dangling from his hand. I gave him a disapproving look, but he returned a look that told me that I couldn't wave this off. I guess there are some procedures that just have to be followed. Just then there was the distinctive clicking sound of a rifle chambering a bullet coming from the side of the saloon.

Brody pounced into action and hoisted his Glock yet again. "Lordy, what now?" he said as he got between us and the new visitor.

"Don't worry about it, Brody," I said in a light-hearted tone. "There's only one person around here who has a lever-action Winchester 1866. *We're over here, Deloris!*"

She came cautiously around the corner of the building and saw that we had things under control. Josie Jones was following right behind her.

"Well you could have told me you'd be outside in this shooting gallery," she groused in her inimitable style. "I was looking all over for you guys until Tully spotted me and sent me out here. Looks like you were right, Merse. Vonnie had Josie locked up in the pantry over there at her place. I saw her run across the lawn heading this way when I rang the doorbell for the umpteenth time, so I knocked on all the windows till I heard Josie hollering."

The Pastor looked mortified. "I…I had no idea. I mean, I figured out that Vonnie had killed Jonesy, but…she was holding Josie in our house? I'm so sorry, Josie…"

Josie looked traumatized, but she managed to speak. "I don't know how I got caught up in Vonnie's big ideas, but she just made everything sound so amazing – and we did have a lot of fun getting out of the house. And now, poor Jonesy is dead!"

Within a few minutes it seemed like the whole town was gathered around us. Tully was out there with his .44

Magnum, and Stan drove right up to the blacksmith shop in his squad car. He took Vonnie into custody, and the others gradually went their own ways. Before long, Brody and I were alone again in the middle of main street in the little western town.

Brody looked at the sky and shielded his eyes from the sun, which was almost directly overhead now. He whistled a little bit of *The Good, the Bad, and the Ugly* and then gave me a steely stare.

"Well, cowgirl," he said in a really macho voice, "I reckon it's about time for that showdown at high noon."

His blue eyes had a hold on me that I was helpless to pull away from.

"On three," he said taking my shoulders in his strong hands. "One…two…" Then he pulled me close and kissed me passionately on the lips. I swear I fell into a world where I could see his heart and mind as we kissed for a prolonged moment. I was still in a stunned silence as our lips gently parted, and my eyes once again locked onto his.

"Lunch?" he asked.

I nodded and took his arm with my both of my hands. "I'm starving!"

We walked slowly back to the car as I savored this moment, which I knew was the beginning of something special. Then he looked at me with his impish grin.

"Well, Mercy Howard – ER nurse, business owner,

sharpshooter, and super-sleuth extraordinaire – it seems when you take off your superhero cape, you're a girl!"

I pressed my head against his shoulder as we walked. "Yup." *And you're a man.* "Well, you know, Brody – a big lady, woman-girl." Hey, I didn't want to lose my feminist card, but I was sure feeling like a girl at the moment.

He smiled. "My favorite kind."

Epilogue

Saturday morning at the Old School Diner was the busiest I'd seen it since my Grand Opening. I think everyone in Paint Creek was there.

"Keep the coffee coming, Deloris!" Babs hollered cheerfully as she set the empty pot on the counter after her round of refills.

"I'm a waitress, not a magician, Babsy" Deloris bellyached with a hint of a smile on her lovely face, setting down a full pot and taking the empty one.

"Hey, beautiful," Red said to Deloris, "where's my flapjacks?"

"And my omelet!" Jake added.

"And my double-everything Lumberjack Breakfast with apple pie!" Junior chimed in. "I sure am hungry."

The smoke alarm went off, and a grey cloud came billowing out of the pass-through window.

Deloris chuckled to herself. "Looks like it's going to be a while, boys. Here's some more coffee."

Pastor D'Arnaud came in the door, wondering what kind of welcome he would receive now that his wife was a known murderer. The dining room did quiet down for a brief moment, but then Babs gave him a warm greeting and a big hug. The chatter and clinking of silverware on china went right back to normal. He looked around for a seat, but the place was full.

"Come with me, Pastor," I said, taking his arm and leading him to a booth that had one side open. Josie Jones was sitting alone on the other side. The Pastor was nervous when he saw her, but Josie smiled and graciously nodded for him to sit down.

"You two have to figure out what to do with that butcher shop," I said with a smile. "I'm getting a lot of complaints on the breakfast sausage I've been using lately, and it would great if we could get things back to normal. I'll send Babs over…"

"Here's coffee and a menu for you Pastor." Babs swooped in with a full cup and topped off Josie's. "The usual, Pastor? Or would you like a menu?"

He sighed. "Time for a fresh start. Let me see a menu, please, Babs."

I walked back to the counter with Babs, and she whispered, "They make a really cute couple, don't they, Mercy!"

I looked at her. "It's a little early for that, Babs. She just lost her husband, and his wife is going to prison for murdering him – or maybe to a state psych ward."

She picked up a hot order that Delois had ready for her. "It's never too early to spend some time with a warm, wonderful person to help heal a hole in your heart, Mercy. The rest of it will come naturally – just you watch and see."

Maybe she's right. They're both really sweet people. I sat back down with Brody in the small booth by the window.

"We'd better stand at the end of the counter and open up this booth for some paying customers," Brody said.

No sooner had we stood up than Ronnie from the hardware store came in, carrying a pink toolbox. "Morning, Mercy! How's that new latch working out for your little critters?"

"Oh! It's really perfect, Ronnie. Thank you so much for doing that. I don't have to cut myself on jagged metal anymore." I motioned for him to sit in the small booth and took the pink toolbox. "This is so sweet of you to bring me one for the diner. I've already used the screwdrivers at home to put new blinds in the bedroom."

Deloris came around took the toolbox from me. "That's going right behind my counter, Mercy. The maintenance crew around here leaves a lot to be desired, so now I'll be able to fix things myself."

Ronnie looked a little taken aback, but I just waived it off and whispered to him, "That just means she's having a good day!"

The door opened one more time.

"Arnie! You finally made it in here!"

"Oh, I'm not here to eat, Mercy. Tommy's waiting for me outside...but we'll be back for lunch. Promise! I just came to give you these," he said dangling my shiny

Mercedes car keys in front of me.

"Oh, my gosh!" I gave Brody an excited look, then I grabbed the keys and gave Arnie a big hug. I probably smelled like motor oil now, but that was okay. "My car is ready!"

Arnie stepped away from the door and motioned his head toward the glass. "There weren't any parking spots right out front, so it's there, across the street."

It was shiny and clean and seemed to glisten in the sunlight. I could almost hear angels singing. Yeah, I really love that car. I turned to Brody and hopped up and down like a giddy child. "Let's go!"

We headed out the door. "Thanks, Arnie! I'll stop by soon so you can run my credit card!"

"You better bring a couple of them cards, Mercy…"

Nothing was going to put a damper on my day now, and I pulled Brody across the street at a full run. The convertible top was down, so I hopped over the door and started it up.

"Where are we going?" he asked as he buckled up.

"Somewhere where there aren't any cops to give me a speeding ticket. Any ideas?"

"There's a seven-mile straight-away on Highway 42. But keep it under 90 or I won't be able to do anything if you get caught."

"90 will do just fine, Brody," I said as I pulled away from the curb. I could really feel the power of my little car. "42 is this way, so at least I won't have to make an illegal U-turn to get there," I chided.

Finally we were cruising with the wind in our hair.

"So, Mercy, how exactly did you figure out that Vonnie was the killer? I was kind of leaning toward the Pastor, especially when he was holding you hostage."

"So was I, because I saw a blue-green car leave Jonesy's in a hurry when we were all out there after the murder, and then I learned it was the Pastor's car when Arnie was working on it. But everything didn't fit, especially when you told me he always drives the little red car."

"Yeah, there was certainly no evidence to take to the D.A."

"And when we were at Tully's you said something about a sweater hanging on the coat rack by the door at Josie's house. I mean, people don't usually use the rack by the door for their own sweaters. Jackets, yes, but not sweaters so much…"

"Mercy…"

"And I knew that Vonnie often wore sweaters, so…"

"Mercy…"

"So, I started to think it might be her. Some of the pieces, like the hammer, I didn't have worked out yet, but…"

"Mercy…"

"What is it, Brody?"

"The sweater that was hanging on Josie's coat rack…"

"Yeah?"

"That's the same sweater she was wearing in the diner this morning. It's her sweater, not Vonnie's."

"So…like…when I took the Pastor's hand off me at the blacksmith shop…"

"Yeah…he still could have been the killer, when you rule out that evidence."

"Oh…well, he wasn't."

"No, he wasn't…and you figured out the real killer."

It was a little unnerving, but everything worked out well. If I hadn't been so sure that the Pastor wasn't the killer, he might have a bullet in his head now, and everything would be so much different today. I decided to change the subject.

"So, Brody…what are we going to do about…"

"Us? That kiss? The undeniable attraction between us that we can't get enough of?"

I looked straight ahead at the road and nodded.

He leaned a little closer and put his hand on my shoulder. My whole body tingled. I looked at the speedometer, and we were at a very reasonable 77 mph.

"Well…" He ran his fingers through my hair just a little. "…after the situational, emotional, and romantic bonding we experienced yesterday, I would say that you're my girl now."

We were silent for a moment, and he put his hand back on my shoulder. I reached up and covered his hand with mine. It seemed so natural, and I knew he was exactly right.

*****

Smoke's Meatloaf

Ingredients:

1 pound ground sausage
2 pounds ground hamburger
2 eggs beaten
1 large onion chopped
8 to 10 saltine crackers crushed
1 teaspoon salt
½ teaspoon pepper
1 red bell pepper, diced fine

1 Tablespoon Worcestershire sauce
½ cup ketchup
8 oz. can tomato sauce

Mix sausage, hamburger, eggs, onion, salt, pepper, red bell pepper, Worcestershire sauce and ketchup in a large mixing bowl. Add the crushed saltine crackers to the meat mixture. Add more crushed crackers if needed to form a tight loaf. Spread the tomato sauce over the top of the loaf.

Place the loaf in a greased 9x5 loaf pan. Bake at 350 degrees for 1 hour or until the meat loaf is done. Allow the loaf to cool for 15 to 20 minutes after removing from the oven. Cooling the loaf will make it easier to slice. Enjoy!

This Recipe is from my Grandmother…Lorene Forgey

Chocolate Fudge Cake

Ingredients:

2 cups sifted flour
3 teaspoons baking powder
½ teaspoon baking soda
¼ teaspoon salt
½ cup butter
1 cup sugar
2 egg yolks, beaten
3 squares Baker's unsweetened chocolate
1 ¼ cups milk

1 teaspoon vanilla
2 egg whites, stiffly beaten

Combine the flour, baking powder, baking soda and salt. Sift together 3 times. Cream the butter, then add sugar gradually. Mix together until light and fluffy. Add the egg yolks and chocolate. Then add the flour and milk alternately adding just a little at a time to the mixture. Beat after each addition until smooth. Add vanilla and fold in the egg whites.

Bake in two greased 9 inch layer pans at 350 degrees for 25 to 30 minutes. Allow the cakes to cool on a wire rack before removing from the pans.

Icing

Ingredients:

3cups powdered sugar
2/3 cup cocoa
1 stick butter
1 teaspoon vanilla
4 to 5 tablespoons heavy cream

Sift the sugar and cocoa together into a large bowl. Combine 1 cup of the sugar and cocoa mixture with the butter and 1 tablespoon of the heavy cream. Beat until smooth. Add another cup of the sugar mixture and another tablespoon or two of cream, beating the mixture until smooth. Add the remaining sugar mixture and cream and beat well. Beat in the vanilla. Add more heavy cream, a tablespoon at a time, if needed to get the consistency you want. Spread the icing over the cakes.

Thanks for reading!

Please submit your honest review on Amazon. Your feedback is important to us!
Book #2 of **The Jessie Delacroix Mystery Series** will arrive on Amazon in early December.
• • • • • • •

To find the entire **Constance Barker** Collection, please visit her <u>Author Page</u>.

Sign up for Constance Barker's <u>New Releases Newsletter</u> to find out when her next book is coming out.

Visit Constance on <u>Facebook</u> to give your personal feedback on the characters and their stories – and get a personal reply from the author.

All of Constance Barker's books are available for

free with Kindle Unlimited.

Take a look at Constance Barker's <u>Best Selling</u>
Caesar's Creek Mystery Series:

<u>A Frozen Scoop of Murder</u> (Caesar's Creek Mystery
Series Book One)

<u>Death by Chocolate Sundae</u> (Caesar's Creek Mystery
Series Book Two)

<u>Soft Serve Secrets</u> (Caesar's Creek Mystery Series
Book Three)

<u>Ice Cream You Scream</u> (Caesar's Creek Mystery
Series Book Four)

<u>Double Dip Dilemma</u> (Caesar's Creek Mystery Series
Book Five)

<u>Melted Memories</u> (Caesar's Creek Mystery Series
Book Six)

<u>Triple Dip Debacle</u> (Caesar's Creek Mystery Series
Book Seven)

<u>Whipped Wedding Woes</u> (Caesars Creek Mystery
Series Book Eight)

And Constance Barker's <u>Best Selling</u> *Sweet Home*
Mystery Series:

Made in the USA
Middletown, DE
28 August 2024

59942428R00085